The Girl and the Guardian

The Oliver Anderson Trilogy, Book One

A Biblical Fiction

by

Joshua D. Jones

The Girl and the Guardian,

The Oliver Anderson Trilogy, Book One

© Joshua D Jones 2020

First Edition
ISBN 978-0-578-77774-0

Cover and interior illustrations by Anthony DePietro of Depietrodraws.com
Cover designed by Stephen Melniszyn of Stephen Melniszyn Designs.
Bible citations from the ESV translation.

'Beauty will save the world.'

\- Dostoevsky

Dedicated: To my daughters.

Note to Readers: Though much of this book is fiction or fantasy, it is based on the ancient epic of Esther as found in Hebrew and Christian Scriptures and serves as the basis for the Jewish holiday of Purim. Connect with other readers on social media with the #GirlAndGuardian hashtag.

Thanks: To Imogen Lowe, Deborah Tardivo, and Gareth Thompson for your proofreading and feedback on the manuscript, I am much obliged. Also, thanks to my family for supporting me in the time it took to write this.

1

532 BC
Babylon

THE WINTER RAIN beat rhythmically on the clay tiles that capped the sacred stone tower. The mages inside had journeyed to Babylon to entomb their deceased leader and discuss the future of their order.

'He was never one of us. Not exactly.' Melchor mumbled.

'Watch your tongue!' Balthasar scolded him. 'He was our chief. Who among us was wiser?'

'He was unique, I'll give him that. But now that he's cold dead, we can practice our art without his corrupting Jewish influence.'

'His magic did things ours couldn't.'

A voice rang out. 'Good evening, brothers! Welcome, please gather round.' Jasper, the mage over their Babylonian chapter, lifted the blue hood from off his shaven head. The torchlight was weak, but it was sufficient to reveal the severe expression on his face. 'I have summoned you here tonight to share important news.'

'Don't keep us waiting, Jasper,' Melchor protested. 'What is it? This meeting isn't a gathering we agreed upon at the outset of our week. Some of us made plans for this evening.'

'Sorry to disrupt your delicate social agendas ladies,' Jasper replied with scorn towards the disagreeable mage. 'I know it's impromptu, but yesterday something fell into my possession, and duty demands that I share. It is,' Jasper cleared his raspy throat, 'a letter from Daniel.' Chatter sparked at the mention of their dead leader. Jasper held up a clay tablet. 'Before he died, he dictated this letter for our order.'

'A letter? About what?'

'It's a prophecy about an ancient evil—and an unexpected rescuer.'

2

Present Day
Scottish Highlands

'YE STARE INTO that thing like it's revealin' the meaning of life.'

Oliver registered that his grandfather had spoken to him. He looked up from his laptop and removed an earbud. 'Sorry, grandad. I was listening to music.'

William smiled at his grandson. 'Nevermind, laddie. How's yer project goin'?'

'It's not going. I've got zero inspiration.'

'How long have ye been workin' on it?'

'Three weeks.'

'What seems to be the problem?'

'When I began this school, I had dreams. I wanted to make productions that moved people. Now it seems like every film and script is the same. I don't see the point.'

'All a bit meaningless?'

'Exactly. And on a practical note, if I don't have a draft ready by Tuesday, I don't think I'll pass.'

3

At nineteen, Oliver Anderson was in his first year at London Film School. He had ploughed right through his first two courses, but this last one, scriptwriting, was challenging his abilities and he had lost focus of why film and theatre had ever attracted him in the first place. The best script would be used for the school production. But Oliver? He just wanted to pass.

His grandfather, William, hearing of Oliver's woes, invited him to spend a few days up at his cabin in the Scottish Highlands. Oliver accepted and took the long and taxing train ride up north—hoping he would find inspiration far from the busy British capital.

He had arrived the night before and was now sitting at grandpa Anderson's kitchen table. He had managed to get dressed and open his laptop, but no fountains of creativity were, as of yet, unleashed.

'Might ye be wantin' some coffee?'

'Sure. Milk, frothy if possible. A shot of caramel syrup will be great—two sugars if you don't have it,' Oliver rattled off without looking up.

William stroked his long white beard and looked at his grandson with a raised eyebrow. 'Maybe that's coffee for a Londoner, but it's not how we do things in Scotland. Here, what ye described is a dessert—and a woman's dessert at that. I'll give it to ye black as the Earl of Hell's waistcoat.'

Oliver looked up in amusement. William noticed. 'That's an expression here for when—'

'Something's really black. Yeah, I got that. But the other part—the bit about it being a woman's coffee. Isn't that, you know, sexist?'

'Sexist?'

'Yeah, sexist.'

'Is that bad?'

'Well, yeah, grandpa. It is.'

'What does it mean?'

'What does what mean?'

'Sexist. What do you think that word means?' William said over his shoulder as he poured the liquid midnight into two enamel mugs.

'Don't you know what it means?'

'Oh, I hear people usin' it. But I'm not convinced most know what they're talkin' about.'

'Well, it means, you know, to treat men and women differently.'

'And that's bad, huh?'

'Absolutely!'

'So ye don't treat men and women differently?'

'No.'

'Really?'

'Yes, really.'

'Okay, ye live in London. What would ye do if yer walkin' home alone from the pub at two in the mornin', and two men followed ye close behind?'

'I'd run—or find a busy street.'

5

'What if two girls were followin' ye?'

'Probably nothing. Unless they were gorgeous—then I might start flirting.'

'It sounds like yer sexist too.'

'How?'

'Yer treatin' men and women differently, aren't ye?'

'That's not how it works.'

'Would ye kiss a beautiful woman?'

'Always.'

'Would ye kiss a big, bearded lad?'

'Never.'

'Ye can call it sexist. I call it common sense.'

'I don't think you understand what I'm trying to say, grandpa.'

'Aye. Perhaps. But I'm not sure ye do either,' William said as he laid one of the steaming cups next to the laptop. 'There's milk in the fridge if ye need it,' he said in a concessionary tone. 'Anythin' else I can get ye?'

'No. Thanks, grandpa. Sorry if I sounded, I dunno—'

'Like a Londoner?'

'Something like that. It's this project—it stresses me out and then it deflates me. I start with an idea, but it goes nowhere. I need inspiration for something beautiful.'

'Beautiful, huh?'

'Yes. But all my ideas are so superficial—they're recycled and dated. I have no desire to fill the world with more pointless words.'

The Girl and the Guardian

William nodded. 'Men find inspiration in different things: a bonnie lass, a wee dram of whisky, prayer. I'm a fan of all three myself.'

Oliver chuckled. Having grown up in the south of England, Oliver didn't know his grandpa William as well as he'd like—but he found his gruff and direct manner endearing. He was different from his own father in several ways, one of them being his faith. 'I know about women. I know about whisky. But I know next to nothing about prayer or the Scriptures.'

'I'm not sure ye know as much about the first two as ye think, laddie. I can give ye advice about women. I can show ye my old casks and let ye experience the second. But the third, the Scriptures, yes, perhaps that's what ye need at the moment.'

Oliver smirked. 'You think some dead prophets will help me with my project?'

'I know little about the technical parts of script writin', *per se*. But I've told lots of stories from the ancient scriptures over the years.'

Oliver sipped the coffee and tried not to wince at its bitter burn. 'I never thought of a man of faith as a storyteller. But I'm not sure the Scriptures would have much inspiration for me. I want to write a play that a London audience can relate to.'

'Maybe it's worth listenin' before ye dismiss the idea.'

'That's fair, and frankly, I'm desperate. Are there many stories in the Scriptures? Isn't it mostly filled with, you know, rules and morals?'

'Is that all yer dad taught you?'

7

'You know dad. He's not into that stuff.'

'Well, yer dad is my son, so I have to assume a bit of responsibility there.'

'I've visited a church at Christmas before. I remember that story: shepherds with towels on their head, baby in a manger—all that. I also celebrated Purim with some Jewish friends. Now that was a blast!'

'Purim, huh? That gives me an idea for a story. Perhaps, if ye sit back and listen, I'll tell it to ye and see if it stirs yer creative juices.'

'I'm willing to try it.'

'Get comfortable. I think I know just the story.'

Oliver leaned back in his chair. William took a gulp of coffee, let out a deep breath, and began.

The Girl and the Guardian

3

471 BC
Susa, Persia

BLOOD RAN DOWN the stone-paved streets and around the mauled hunks of humanity that had decorated the ancient lanes and passages since dawn. Every building surrounding the Jewish quarter belched out violence. Enemies assailed from all directions. The war cries of thousands, the screams of horses, and the clashing of metal all blended in an apocalyptic symphony. For the ones trapped inside those narrow walkways, it sounded like the end of the world. Only louder.

But the children of Zion stood against the darkness. In Susa, and throughout the Persian Empire, they fought to protect their neighbours and children from an evil determined to butcher and pillage. Even from the palace, the Queen could hear the clash and clatter of weapons climbing up out of the city. Her right hand tightened its grasp on the dagger sheathed by her side. Usually, she would never think to carry a weapon. But today was the dreaded thirteenth day of Adar. Today, even a bodyguard could slice her throat and not be legally culpable.

9

She squeezed the hand of the man to her left. 'Will our forces hold?'

A kiss dropped onto her myrrh scented forehead. 'Peace. We prepared our people for this day, and a merciful heaven battles alongside us.'

This man had rescued the Queen from despair more than once with his words of hope. She relaxed her grip and whispered a prayer upward—thankful for the miracle that had prepared her people to fight back against this genocide.

But will it be enough?

A hurricane of circumstances had spun her life from orphan to Empress. For a while, she had even lost the man she now stood beside. Then, he was her guardian. Now, she was his Queen.

For today, however, she just wanted to survive the genocide.

The Girl and the Guardian

4

OLIVER OPENED HIS eyes. 'Wait! What are you telling me?'

'I'm elaboratin' a Scripture story.'

'This story is in the Scriptures? Like, the Bible? It sounds like Arabian Nights just met the Third Reich.'

'Well, some of the Biblical Scriptures take place in Persia.'

'Okay. But this is murder and genocide.'

'Ye don't know much about the Bible, do ye?'

'No, I suppose I don't. Still, it's not what I expected.'

'Should I start again?'

'Well, I feel like I'm missing something. Who are these people?'

'I guess I jumped right in.'

'I'm here for four days, so I've got time. Can you start from the beginning?'

'No problem.'

'I think this Scripture story won't be completely dull.'

'I'm sure the writers of Scripture would take yer words as a deep compliment. I suppose if we're going to have a proper beginning, I should start by setting the scene.'

The Oliver Anderson Trilogy

5

'MEAT AND BREAD for two siglos!' a man wielding a carving knife yelled.

'Have your future told for four siglos!' a mage in green robes shouted.

'Enjoy an hour of love and pleasure for six siglos!' a woman plastered in makeup called.

Spices and perfume burned the nostrils. Imperial fire pits raged to barbeque meat for an army while harlots erected tents on every street corner. Dancers, musicians, artists, and aspiring magi from throughout the Empire flocked to the city to inflate everyone's understanding of what a party could be. The Persians had to celebrate. They were preparing for war.

Susa was a city that dropped jaws even under normal conditions. It was the capital of Susiana, and one of the four glorious capitals of the Persian Empire. Susa, a name that meant 'lily', was a city with a youthful face, but old eyes. Though the Persians modernised it with additional features, they couldn't hide its ancient qualities.

It wasn't only the city's buildings. The girls of Susa also had a reputation for being exceptionally beautiful. When Alexander the Great later conquered the city, Susa was the one place army commanders allowed mass weddings—that's how many soldiers had fallen for local girls. That this capital was now in continual party mode only robed the elegant city in decadence.

But something was rotten in the state of Susiana. Cyrus the Great, the father of the Persian Empire, was long dead, and some whispered that the principled leniency and generosity that had marked his rule had given way to the forces of moral decay, cruelty, and treason. Internal dissent was growing, and public executions increased as the royal spy network kept sharp ears open for criticism of the Empire's leadership.

The lavish party covered Susa's ugliness—but only superficially. People complain less about a government when it gives them meat, wine, magic, and sex in abundance. But death is an ugliness no government can hide. Rulers may establish good policies that help people extend their lives a few more years. But the death rate is always the same in every nation: one per person. Despite the celebrations that circulated in the city streets, death still knocked on a door in Susa's Jewish quarter.

***

The wail of mourners contrasted against the rhythms and beats of Susa's atmosphere. Death had visited a home and taken a middle-aged grocer.

The passing was unexpected. Abihail had been an active participant in the local synagogue and devout in his prayers. He had also been in excellent health. The physician was still unsure what caused it, though some speculated that produce from one of the stranger parts of the Empire had poisoned him. He had taken ill five days previously. At first, the doctor had assumed it was a virus and had ordered him to rest and drink plenty of broth. But after three days, Abihail deteriorated, and the anxious doctor could do nothing to stop his expiry.

Four synagogue elders stood in the middle of the house and spoke with each other amidst the wailing. They stroked their beards—two black and two grey—and cast an occasional eye at the child in the corner. The black-haired girl sat still, clutching her doll, and staring at the wall.

'The closest relative is in Israel—the mother's sister.'

'I thought the mother died in childbirth?'

'She did. Abihail raised the girl himself.'

'Are there no other relatives left in Susa?'

'Only three. One is an older widow who I doubt has the strength to take on a child. The second is a married woman. Unfortunately, an accident left her husband disabled, and the couple relies on synagogue charity to pay rent as it is.'

'What about the third?'

'Well, see for yourself. He's the young man coming through the door—right there.'

'Him? What's his name?'

'Mordecai, son of Jair.'

The Girl and the Guardian

'How's he related? A young uncle?'

'No, her older cousin.'

'Is he married?'

'Not yet. But he has a respectable career that pays well. He could at least provide for her.'

'Adoption by a male cousin isn't ideal.'

'These aren't ideal times.'

'Would he be willing?'

'I believe Mordecai was close to his uncle. Did you see how he flew up the stairs to Abihail's room as soon as he came through the door?'

'We can ask. If he says no, we must find someone to take the girl to relatives in Israel.'

'Before we ask him, let's pray. Heaven lays plans for every life. He cares as much for this orphan in the corner as cares for King Xerxes on his throne.'

The eyes of one of the younger rabbis flashed. 'Even more! She is of Israel. The King is a Gentile! It's not right that she mourns her father, heartbroken beyond words, while the King continues to get drunk at the citadel with his concubines.'

'I'll not debate either Heaven's justice or the value of Persian lives with you tonight, Isaac,' the elder rabbi said in mild rebuke. 'Can we at least agree to pray for this girl's future before we approach her cousin?'

The Oliver Anderson Trilogy

6

IN THE CENTRE of the city, the King vomited up his food and returned to the garden table with a proud stride. 'Another jug!' He commanded his servants with a shout. The King guzzled wine with as much gusto as he lusted after the girls who carried it to him.

On the outside, Ahasuerus was successful in all the ways men judge success. He stood tall and handsome—one of the reasons his father Darius had chosen him as successor. He ruled 50 out of the world's 112 million people in an empire that stretched from India to Ethiopia. The King of kings had glory, good-looks, power, wealth, and women—in quantities beyond all measure.

On the inside, as is often the case with those on the high places of society's success ladder, things were not so glorious. Better known by his Greek name, Xerxes, he was—regarding his rage, alcohol, food, lust, and depression issues—one of Adam's more dysfunctional sons. And, as the King, he indulged these dysfunctions without anyone to restrain him.

Xerxes was the new Emperor of Persia's Achaemenid dynasty. He took over at age thirty-three in 486 BC when some whispered that the Empire he ruled was going downhill. King Darius and the Persian army had attempted to take mainland Greece a few years earlier but had their arses handed to them unexpectedly by the small city-state of Athens and its allies. It was an international embarrassment that Xerxes was determined to remedy. Morale depended on it. In the second year of his reign, he began preparing to avenge his father's failure. How would he start?

He'd do so with a party.

Though inaugurating a military crusade with a debauched celebration was standard Persian practice, Xerxes elevated his party to stratospheric heights. He called soldiers from throughout his Empire to come to Susa and celebrate his glory.

'What do we have, Memucan?'

'Your Majesty, we have Assyrian warriors with their maces, Cissians in their turbans, Moschians with their wooden helmets, Ethiopian archers dressed in leopard-skins, and the Indians who wield tall bows and are wearing what they call baggy dhotis—a bit strange to my eyes.'

'They are my glory. Let them feast!'

Having been queuing elsewhere when the angels distributed the gift of moderation, the Great King's party was, in fact, historic. There had never been one like it. Luxuries were beyond counting. Purple fabric, from a dye so rare it was the mark of royal clothing, now dressed the city's avenues. 'Make the wine

17

and food limitless for everyone,' he declared to the event planners. 'Let everyone indulge their appetites as much as they like.'

'For how long, Your Majesty?'

'For six months.'

Eat. Drink. Vomit. Repeat. It was extravagant. It was reckless. It was Xerxes. The King then followed this six-month party with a week-long drinking celebration in the palace garden—this was the party after the party. The Ancient Persian word for these lavish gardens was 'pardis'—from where we get 'paradise'. This post-party was for everyone who wanted to come, even those from the lower classes. Silver bowls filled with wine were so plentiful, one might get drunk by merely breathing the air. The King set up golden sofas so that his guests could nap when they wearied from feasting.

He meant it to be Heaven on earth—a utopia where he could enjoy his greatness. On the last day of the party, however, the whole thing shattered like an old clay pot against a stone when his Queen refused a royal request.

The Girl and the Guardian

[The King] gave a feast for all his officials and servants. The army of Persia and Media and the nobles and governors of the provinces were before him, while he showed the riches of his royal glory and the splendour and pomp of his greatness for many days, 180 days.
And when these days were completed, the king gave for all the people present in Susa, the citadel, both great and small, a feast lasting for seven days in the court of the garden of the king's palace.
-Esther 1

The Oliver Anderson Trilogy

7

'WHOA! SUSA SOUNDS like Vegas meets Beijing: debauched and authoritarian,' Oliver cut in.

'What'd ye expect? Narnia?'

'I expected a virtuous city with a just King—you know, with it being in the Bible, shouldn't it read more like a fairy-tale?'

'Susa wasn't exactly, as ye might say, family-friendly in the 5th Century BC. It was dark. Evil, like a parasite, was suckin' the life from all the strong and the good within her. But that doesn't mean God's not present. He does beautiful things, even in the ugliest of places.'

'In art class, we'd often use a dark backdrop to highlight something beautiful. Is it like that?'

'Somethin' along those lines. Redemption is the big fancy word for it.'

'Many of the stories I come across either have a trite happy ending, or else they get continually darker or more hopeless.'

'True redemption is neither trite nor hopeless. It deals with real darkness, but it doesn't leave it that way. In this story, the tools of that redemption will be a girl and her guardian.'

The Girl and the Guardian

'Not all beauty needs darkness; does it?'

'Perhaps not always. But let's use words precisely. How do ye define beauty?'

'Beauty? Um, you know, something that looks good.'

'That's a start, I suppose. Beauty dances too wildly for ye to pin it down to a textbook definition. But one thing ye can say about genuine beauty is that it's self-evident.'

'Meaning?'

'Meaning ye know when ye experience it. Ye might ask, "Why is the music of bagpipes or the sight of a sunset from the highest peak of Ben Nevis beautiful?" The best response is, "Listen. Look. They are." Beautiful sights, sounds, and smells all have something in common: yer pleased when ye perceive 'em.'

Oliver nodded thoughtfully. 'I'd never thought of that. Yeah, I guess they all make us happy when we pay attention to them.'

'Discoverin' what true beauty is has been the business of great thinkers all through history. It wasn't until the dawn of the modern era that we marginalised the subject.'

'I'm guessing the Bible says something about beauty?'

'Aye. The Bible teaches that beauty's a gift from God—that it flows from his nature. It's a special gift he's given us humans to enjoy.'

'Don't animals enjoy it too?'

'Not like us. Ye can value beauty in a way that beasts can't. I don't mean that they can't see or hear somethin' capable of grabbin' their attention. But this only fulfils some biological urge to eat or mate. A bird may see a bright red berry and desire

21

it for food. A male grouse may give a seductive matin' call that attracts a female grouse. Get it?'

'Yeah, I see what you mean. For animals, it's biological intuition driven by their need to survive.'

'Exactly. But ye and I can appreciate beauty for its own sake with no connection to survival. Ye can cherish the beauty of a sunset, a paintin', a song, or a bonnie lass—all having nothing to do with nutrition or reproduction. We enjoy it for its own sake.'

'And you think God made all this? For us?'

'Aye. If ye don't believe that God created it, what other options are ye left with?'

'The Big Bang.'

'That's all good and fine. But if there's no God behind that bang, then chance and chaos take over everythin'. Beauty becomes a mere freak accident of the universe.'

'Yeah, I guess so. A lucky accident?'

'How can ye declare somethin' to be beautiful if yer nothing more than random stardust flying through the universe? Only if ye acknowledge a Creator can beauty make sense and this world have real meanin'—otherwise it's all a big mishap.'

'Worth thinking over. But can we get back to the story now, grandpa?'

'Right. Where was I?—oh yeah, the reckless King. I guess we need to talk about the Queen.'

The Girl and the Guardian

8

'A WORD FROM the King, Your Majesty.' Hathach, one of the King's messenger-eunuchs, bowed and extended a written message to her royal hand.

'What does that pompous baboon want now?' The Queen asked with a fatigued eye-roll.

'Top beauty' is what Vashti's name means in Old Persian—and she lived up to the name. Some women change the air in the room merely by entering it. This delicious slice of paradise was not only such a woman, but she was a woman who knew she was such a woman. Vashti believed that other women wished they were her. Usually, she was right. With striking looks, a stellar education, and royal blood flowing through her veins, she was used to getting whatever she desired.

She had desired to marry the Emperor. He possessed more power than any other man, plus he was handsome—two qualities which made it easy for her to overlook his impulsive nature. Marrying him increased her own majesty and made her half of the ultimate power couple in the world.

The Oliver Anderson Trilogy

Now she wanted her King of kings to stop annoying her with his new ideas. For six months she helped throw his 'greatest party ever'. She had worked hard and didn't care to serve any more of his royal requests.

Her building resentment climaxed at the end of an evening banquet. Vashti had finished feasting with the aristocratic ladies. She was walking to her quarters when Hathach handed her Xerxes' message:

Darling, this garden party is amazing.
But hey, it's bound to be! I'm the one throwing it!
If you're done with your ladies' meal, then get out here quick!
The entire city has turned up, and most of the commoners have never seen you. I told them all about your radiance!
Compared to you, their wives are trolls.
Hurry, we're waiting!
PS. Don't forget the crown I made for you!

The message failed to impress the Queen. 'Hathach!'

'Yes, Your Majesty. How shall I respond?'

'Tell my husband I wasn't born with enough middle fingers to respond adequately. I've taken my shoes off. I have three tiring sons to care for—and you know how much trouble little Artaxerxes is to get to bed. Tell him he can enjoy his party without me.'

Hathach hesitated. 'But, Your Majesty, this is the King!'

'Even on the world's highest throne, there's still nothing but an arse. You know I'm not against turning some heads—but not

The Girl and the Guardian

for a stinking mob of commoners. Tell the King to get one or two of his concubines with a nice rack to show off to the masses. I'm off to bed.'

'Your Majesty, harem girls isn't what he wants. The King desires your royal company. I don't think—'

'It is not your job to think, is it Hathach? It's your job to deliver messages. Now, I'm sorry you have to serve the son of an upstart lance-bearer. Less than a century earlier, these Persians were only a backward vassal state. I was born into a proper royal lineage—one in which the women do not flaunt their beauty in front of shopkeepers and bakers!'

Hathach bowed again. 'I'll convey your message, Your Majesty.' And he did. To what effect? First, Xerxes felt embarrassed; then offended; then angry. He may not have been as self-controlled as his ancestors, but authority was one principle that he understood and valued.

The King's heart roared. *If an Emperor's own wife won't obey him, who will obey him?!* He sought words to minimise the embarrassment, 'Sorry everyone. Forget what I said earlier. The Queen will not be coming out to greet you. It seems she has a headache.'

Oh?

***

The next morning, the sobered King was in a mood for action. 'Hathach, call for Memucan, the magi, and the other royal advisors!'

'As you wish, Your Majesty.'

The King's trusted advisors gathered about him and he disclosed to them the embarrassment of the night before. 'What should we do in response to the Queen's conduct?'

A leading mage stepped forward. 'The stars speak of mystery and reversal. Destiny will lift up some and bring down others. A great exchange will come.'

Xerxes took a moment to muse on what those mystic words might mean, then he asked, 'How about you, legal scholars?'

A lawyer approached the throne. 'The Persian King is, according to the code of the Medes and the Persians, perfect and divine. To refuse him is to refuse Heaven.'

'So, what must I do with my Queen?' Xerxes asked, turning to his chief counsellors.

Memucan spoke for the group. 'If Vashti's rebellion goes unpunished, other women will join her disobedience! We must remove from her position before the cancer spreads.'

'Removed? As in death?' Xerxes asked with a raised eyebrow.

'Either that or banishment, Your Majesty.'

Xerxes considered the issue. The Queen's refusal had wounded his pride, but he had loved her. It hadn't just been political. Not for him. The thought of her execution was too much for his tastes. 'Banishment, it shall be. Take her from the throne this very day.'

The Girl and the Guardian

9

'GRANDPA?'

William raised an eyebrow. 'Another interruption?'

'Sorry,' Oliver said sheepishly from across the table. 'But, could the King do that? Kick out the Queen? It doesn't seem fair.'

'The ancient Persian world would care little for yer 21st Century notions of fair. Plus, it sets the story up for another Queen that's comin'—one that, in contrast to Vashti, is bonnie both inside and out.'

'What was Vashti's problem?'

'She was proud.'

'What's wrong with that? Everyone needs a bit of pride.'

'I know that's popular in yer generation to say. It was, to a degree, even in mine. But that's not what the sacred stories teach. Rather, they say 'God resists the proud but gives grace to the humble.' The Bible depicts pride as being Satanic. Ye see, Satan was one of the most beautiful archangels—but the true King banished him because of his pride.'

'Harsh.'

The Oliver Anderson Trilogy

'Not if ye understand the root of pride. Pride believes that we can have true and lastin' beauty without God. Thinkin' that our glory depends on ourselves leads to either arrogance or discouragement.'

Oliver looked puzzled. 'How can pride be both arrogance and discouragement?'

'We sometimes trust arrogantly in our genetics, fitness, or fashion. But, at other times, we feel discouraged by these things. We can't lose the weight, build the muscle, or get fit in the way we want. In both cases, whether arrogant or insecure, we depend on ourselves.'

'I get it. I know some girls who, like Vashti, look down on people. But others, even if they're attractive, think they aren't and get depressed. It happens to guys too—maybe not as often.'

'Aye, that's right. But there's another way to relate to beauty—a healthier way. Yer not forced to choose between arrogance and discouragement. The Bible tells us there's another type. It's a beauty that leaves us humbled, encouraged, and happy.'

'Back to the story now?' Oliver asked, betraying his curiosity.

'Yes. Now you need to meet our girl.'

The Girl and the Guardian

10

HADASSAH SWUNG BY Samuel's bakery on the way home from school. The bag she carried already had goat meat from the market, and now all she needed was some bread to accompany her evening dish. Samuel's ovens pumped out tasty loaves, but that wasn't the only reason she went to his bakery. Hadassah came here because talking with Samuel was simple. Samuel was a married man and, though he was friendly, he was not the type to flirt when his wife wasn't around.

Not that Hadassah objected to flirting or a bit of romantically charged attention from eligible men. In fact, she rather enjoyed it. Her current set of circumstances, however, were such that she was trying to avoid getting any more than she already had. Over the last two years, Hadassah had developed a remarkable beauty of both body and face—with eyes that could melt a man like snow tossed into a bonfire.

'Shalom, shalom!' she said, to the baker as she walked in.

'Hadassah! Good to see you. Would you like your usual?'

'Same as always, Sam.'

'Wait a moment. I brought some fresh loaves out of the oven only a moment ago. Let me get you one.'

Hadassah couldn't help but notice Samuel's extra-positive mood. When he returned from the back, carrying a loaf, she said, 'You seem chipper today. Any special occasion? Is business doing well?'

Samuel beamed. 'Chana and I are expecting our second child! Soon little Solomon will have a baby brother or sister!'

'Congratulations! That's such good news.'

'Thank you, Hadassah. I'll tell Chana you said so.'

'Please do,' Hadassah said with a smile.

'And you? I believe you have a birthday coming up? Is that right?'

'I sure do.'

'Am I right in thinking you'll be fifteen?'

'You are.'

'An important year for a girl.'

'Yes, let's hope so. Anyway, please give my love to Chana. I'm so happy for the both of you.'

And Hadassah meant it. But Samuel's good news provoked mixed feelings for her. She had known Chana growing up, and Hadassah was only two years her junior. That she was now three years married, and Hadassah still not engaged, brought back to the forefront of her mind a host of issues—issues she needed to discuss with Mordecai now that she was turning fifteen.

She walked out of the bakery and down the narrow street towards her neighborhood with the bread under her arm. How would she bring all this up with Mordecai? She didn't know. Some of their more recent talks had been heated. Hadassah had been pressing him with questions about returning to the Holy Land—a growing desire fuelled mainly by the views of some teachers at her synagogue school.

It had been about fifty years since Zerubbabel, Joshua the priest, and 50,000 other Jews had returned from throughout the Empire to rebuild Jerusalem. It had also been nearly thirty years since they completed the temple and resumed worship. Some said that to be near Jerusalem was to be near Heaven.

Sometimes, after dinner, when the darkness, food, and wine worked their magic, she would grow bolder, and her questions would leap across the table. 'Why aren't we in Jerusalem?'

'Because this is our home. This is where we were born.'

'But home isn't where you're born. Home is where you belong.'

'Is this what I get for paying for your school? A girl who's smarter than me?' he'd respond with a wink.

'I'm only asking, Morty.'

'I know. Time for bed.'

Their relationship was unique, strong, and capable of handling Hadassah's increasingly adult questions. They hadn't discussed suitors, however. She knew that Mordecai kept them at a distance. A few eligible fellas, brave enough to face Mordecai, had attempted to pursue her—but found their battering ram advances failed to make a dent in Mordecai's iron will. Others, who were not so brave, had courted her only in their fantasies while their eyes followed the heartbreaking sway of her unachievable backside at a safe distance.

For Jews, sending a suitor packing was the right of any guardian. A man could wield discretion over his daughter's readiness to marry. After fifteen, however, Hebrew tradition declared there should be no more delay.

Mordecai was diligent in executing his role as a guardian, and Hadassah guessed he probably had some plan for her future. He had mentored her in Persian culture far beyond what most Jewish girls experienced. He also enrolled her in the synagogue's new school for girls. With a sense of duty resting heavily on his shoulders, he helped her grow into a woman capable of navigating life in a capital city—one with more than a few dangers for pretty girls. For her fourteenth birthday, Mordecai allowed her to begin travelling outside the Jewish quarter without him. But this liberty came with two conditions.

'Here's the dagger I promised you,' he said, holding the weapon firmly in his hand. 'Wear it whenever you venture into the city. Only use it if you are in great need—for I would rather you run away if you face real danger.'

Hadassah stretched out her trembling hand. 'I'll be very careful with it,' she promised with wide eyes.

'I'll give you lessons to ensure you know how to properly wield it. The other condition for venturing outside the neighbourhood is that you use the name of Esther.'

'What? "Esther"? As in "star-child"? What's wrong with my actual name?'

The Girl and the Guardian

'Nothing's wrong with it—it's lovely.'

'Then why "star-child"? Why can't I tell the Persians my name is Hadassah or at least use a Hebrew name?'

'Because privacy is power. What people don't know, they can't destroy. You won't stand out with a name like Esther.'

Hadassah loved the dagger, but she questioned the second name. Some Jews saw the use of a Persian name as an act of unfaithfulness—and Hadassah was becoming sympathetic with that view. It seemed like a compromise of her integrity.

She also found Mordecai's dedication to his citadel career confusing. *Why is my cousin so devoted to serving a drunk, pagan King who sticks his royal sausage in all the wrong aristocratic pantries? Why doesn't he take us home to Israel? Wouldn't there be better suitors there?*

Hadassah didn't know. She knew, however, that they needed to have a talk.

11

HE DARTED OUT of the office and onto the citadel's limestone streets. Mordecai hurried through the gates and towards the Jewish quarter for the café where his friend waited. He was the last to leave. Again. Mordecai loved his job, but the hours ran long. He wanted to share drinks with Jeremiah before going home to eat with his little cousin.

'Hey, rat's fart!' Jeremiah waved from across Babak's noisy café.

Mordecai sat on a pillow and filled his cup. 'Hello, you vomitus pig.'

'A "vomitus pig"? Careful, Morty. I have a weakness for vanity and can be most susceptible to flattery.'

They were best friends.

Babak's café was near the Jewish quarter. He was Persian, but had enough business sense to keep his menu semi-kosher. Candles, pillows, rugs, and banter filled the musty interior. A bowl of pistachios and two wooden cups stood between them, along with a half-empty jug of wine.

'Cheers to you, Morty.'

34

'You're cheering me?' Mordecai laughed. 'What do you want?'

'Come now, I want to work my way through a jug with my best friend. Let the conversation flow where it will.'

'Best friend? Now I know you've got an agenda. I'm afraid you're going to have to order a second jug and, this time, make it a better vintage. This stuff is terrible.'

'Your citadel career has made you a wine snob.'

'Why waste your life drinking a bad vintage? If Heaven gives his people wine, we'd be foolish to not choose the good stuff.'

'Great theology. You a civil servant, bartender, or a Torah teacher?'

Mordecai smiled. 'Maybe, before I die, I shall try all three.'

'A second it is. Anyway, the more I drink, the less dull you become.'

'Ha! So, what is this liquid courage supposed to help us discuss?'

'Hadassah.'

Mordecai was curious. 'Hadassah? Is this about her nationalism?'

'Let's save that one for another time.'

'Oh? What is it then?'

'It's more to do with you and Hadassah—as a pair.'

Mordecai drew back a few inches. 'This doesn't sound good.'

Jeremiah yelled towards the back of the café, 'Babak! Another jug please—and don't dilute! I like water in my baths, not my wine!'

'So, what about her?' Mordecai asked directly.

'She turns fifteen next week.'

Mordecai sensed where this was going, and he wasn't happy about it. 'Gee, thanks for reminding me. I'll pick up a nice present.'

'What are you going to do about her suitors?'

'What suitors?'

'What suitors?! There's a queue!'

Mordecai slapped his cup on the table with more force than he'd intended and wine slushed over his hand. 'So, I've waited. What of it? She was too young. I'm her guardian. I do what I think is best for her.'

'I'm asking about this for your benefit too, you know.'

'How so?'

'Some folks think she's kinda, you know, hot.'

'There's nothing hot about my little cousin!'

'Hearing you say so would thrill her, I'm sure. Okay, let's try "lovely". People find her lovely.'

'Do you?'

'I'm engaged to Miriam!' Jeremiah protested.

'That doesn't answer my question.'

'Do you know how others see her?'

'Meaning?'

'She has a reputation for being the most gorgeous girl in the Jewish quarter. Her hair is like a raven's feather, her personality like the wind, her eyes flash lightning bolts—'

'Is this poetry? Cause it sounds recited.'

'It's how people perceive her. You're her guardian. That means you need to be aware of what's going on.'

'To answer your question, of course. I'm not blind. My cousin has indeed blossomed into one of Job's daughters. When I adopted that awkward nine-year-old six years ago, I had no idea what a knockout she'd become or how many suitors I'd have to push away.'

'Do you regret it?'

'What? Unpack that question for me.'

'I mean, you forfeited the right to marry her when you adopted her. As her cousin, you'd be first in the queue of potential suitors. You're not holding onto her for any reason that might create a scandal, are you?'

'What? No! Definitely not.'

Jeremiah backed away with his hands raised in surrender. 'Okay, I take you at your word. I believe that you believe that. Care to expound any more though?'

'Ah, I see.' Mordecai took a deep breath. 'I'm a man like the rest of them. Yes, I desire the company of a beautiful woman— even if my job doesn't give me the time to get one! Had I known back then what she'd become, would I have done it differently? I don't know. And I don't see any point in wondering. But what else could I have done? My cousin was an orphan, and I vowed to be her guardian. No, I don't regret that. How could I? If that cost me the right to marry the most beautiful Jewish girl of our generation, well, then so be it. I'll find someone else.'

'Excellent. Joy to the world. I'm glad to hear that's not why you've been so overprotective.'

'Overprotective? Have I been? Look, my guardian role includes finding her an appropriate husband—and I'll do what I said I would.'

'You do keep your word. Everyone loves that about you. I never thought you'd run off with Hadassah or anything.'

'So why the questioning?'

Jeremiah grinned. 'It's my job, as a friend, to make you feel uncomfortable.'

'You're good at it. Look, I decided to have a particular type of relationship with Hadassah. I'm her guardian. I'll stick with my choice—and I refuse to harrow my soul with inward interrogations. And let the old lady rumours of this neighbourhood be damned.'

'So, if it's not for anything inappropriate, why isn't Hadassah engaged or married yet?'

'No reason. I've been busy with work.'

'You tell yourself that—and it's partially true. But there's more, isn't there.'

Mordecai took another gulp of his wine. He wanted to be honest with both himself and with Jeremiah. 'I'm not sure. Maybe part of the reason I've dug my feet in is both less scandalous and more pathetic than what the Jewish rumour mill might suggest. You know what it is?'

'I'm listening.'

'I'm starting to enjoy her company. She's no longer a needy child that I'm obliged to raise. She's matured into a good housemate and a friend.'

Jeremiah laughed. 'A friend? Have you become nostalgic? The strong and successful Mordecai? Even if that's true, you'd still be a selfish fart nibbler if you prevent her from marrying.'

'I'll find her a suitable husband after her birthday.'

'Marry her off then get yourself hitched. A wife would keep you company and make you happy.'

'Is that what wives do?'

'Sometimes—or so I hear.'

'Women are fallen humans with us in this shipwrecked world. They're not always guiding stars or endless sources of joy.'

'True. And women aren't cheap! But then, you've got plenty of money.'

'Money doesn't keep you from being lonely.'

'How could you ever be lonely with me as your best friend? I'm amazing company!' Jeremiah proclaimed.

'Of course, you are Jere, I just mean—'

'No offence was taken. I get that you like spending time with Hadassah. She's a far a kinder person than me, and she has a much nicer body to stare at.

'No, Jere—'

'Even if I'm second-place to her, I'll still be here for you.'

'Um, thanks…I think.'

'You need to marry her off to someone soon so you can find a lovely Jewish maiden of your own. Hurry. No girl will marry you if you've got your smoking hot cousin living with you.

'Enough with the "smoking hot" type comments.'

Jeremiah put his hands up in surrender. 'Sue me. I'm a man, and I'm conscious. But don't fear losing Hadassah. We're talking about weddings, not funerals. I'm sure you and your future wife will visit Hadassah and her husband all the time. You'll drink wine, play board games, and travel into middle age as friends.'

'That's a nice thought.'

'I get them occasionally. You should listen to me more— you'd be amazingly wise if you did.'

Mordecai laughed silently, then said, 'Do me a favour. Make sure I'm meeting with suitors by the end of the month. Kick my butt if not.'

'Aye, aye captain! Not that you'll have to look for them. They'll queue up straight after her birthday. Talk frankly with Hadassah before that. Make sure you both agree on what the qualifications should be so that you don't waste time considering sub-par fellas. And, when you both agree that I'd be the perfect husband, let me know. She can be my second wife. I'm sure Miriam wouldn't mind.'

'Anyone ever tell you what a schmuck you are?'

'Besides you? Just my friends and family.'

'I'll talk to her this week. Maybe tonight.'

12

'HADASSAH SOUNDS LIKE a top girl, grandpa. I suppose that's one thing that could get me to believe in God: a gorgeous woman. It's hard to imagine something like that happened by accident.'

'Aye, she was bonnie. The writers of the Bible believed that God wove beauty into our universe. Lots of it. God's purpose, from the first chapter of the Bible, is for everythin' to be beautiful.'

'Why?'

'The beautiful things ye see in creation—the trees, the lochs, the lasses—are there to let us know about God himself.'

'So people of faith believe that God is beautiful?'

'Jewish and Christian teachers have always believed that God's the most beautiful by an infinite degree and that all true beauty flows from him. Ye see, God's beauty surpasses Vashti, Hadassah, and all other beauties the way the light of the sun surpasses the light of a candle. For us, worshippin' God isn't a chore. When ye glimpse God's glory, it is a beauty that takes yer breath away. The beauties of this world, excellent as they may

41

be, always leave us hungry for more. That's because they're not ends in themselves. They point us to our true and forever home.'

'Huh. I never thought of God that way. Can we—'

'Get back to the story? Of course.'

13

MORDECAI HAD LIVED the whole of his twenty-eight years in Susa. His great, great-grandfather had been a Jewish exile from the tribe of Benjamin when the Babylonian King, Nebuchadnezzar, kidnapped many Jews from Jerusalem—a city he went on to destroy. Israel had rebelled against the rule of Heaven, despite the warnings the prophets had given, so Heaven removed its protection and allowed Babylon to bring its destruction. That was 120 years ago. Since then, Babylon had fallen to the Persian Empire at which time Cyrus the Great announced the Jews could return to the small sliver of land on the eastern Mediterranean that Heaven had declared should be forever theirs. Some did, but some stayed.

Mordecai's family lived in Susa. They were sincere in their religious devotion. They often met with other Jews for prayer and Torah reading in what was being called 'synagogues'. Yet his family had also integrated well into broader, Persian society. Their connections through the city helped them to prosper as merchants, and that prosperity allowed them to send their sons to excellent, Persian schools. Mordecai's older brother used his

43

school years to prepare to take over the family business. Mordecai, as the younger of two, had the freedom to pursue something other than the family trade.

Joshua, the grandson of Abednego, the respected and aged Jewish elder, visited his class when he was eleven. Mordecai knew the stories of Heaven's dealings with Abednego, Daniel, and their friends as they worked for the Babylonian government. Listening to the wise and inspiring words of Joshua, now himself a high-level government official, stirred that history to life. Mordecai introduced himself to Joshua after his presentation and, as he was the only Jewish boy in the class, Joshua felt a special connection to him.

Should your son ever need help in the world of Persian government, let me know. I see potential in him, Joshua wrote in a note to Mordecai's parents.

He excelled in school and secured a management-level job in Susa's import division when he was only seventeen. He liked his work and hoped he could turn it into a career.

Five years and one job promotion later, tragedy struck his family. His uncle Abihail, of whom Mordecai was particularly fond, died from an illness. As Abihail was a widower, this made his daughter an orphan a presented Mordecai with an unexpected and challenging choice.

'No one expects you to raise your cousin. It's not normal.' Jeremiah told him.

'These aren't normal times. There are few other relatives left in this city—and fewer still that can afford an extra mouth to feed.'

'Hope you like playing with dolls.'

'This isn't what I planned on, but uncle Abihail was a kind man. Taking guardianship of her is the right thing to do.'

'Better you than me.'

The Oliver Anderson Trilogy

14

'WAIT, SO THIS bloke became the legal guardian of his nine-year-old cousin when he was in his early twenties?!'

William nodded at his grandson. 'Aye. And?'

'That's nuts. I'll be in my early twenties soon. I couldn't do that.'

'Aye. I've noticed it takes young folks a bit longer to grow up than it did in our day. But, presumably, ye've felt the instinct to protect a woman before?'

'Of course!' Oliver insisted. 'I walk friends home from late-night parties.'

'Where d'ya think that instinct comes from?'

'It's common sense. It's a good thing to protect girls in a city like London.'

'Treatin' men and women differently?'

'That again? I'll figure out a good definition of sexism and get back to you, okay?'

'I'm aquiver with anticipation. But, regardin' yer instinct to protect yer lady friends, to be a guardian is a task that resonates deep within a man's soul. The Bible tells how God gave the first

46

man a two-part job: to cultivate and to guard the garden that he had put him in. The guardin' instinct was in man's heart before sin. Ye can still see it in young boys when they play superheroes or in young men who enlist when their country goes to war.'

'But isn't war bad?' Oliver asked.

'It's worse than bad. It's horrific. Evil! But if yer a genuine soldier, ye don't go to war because ye hate what's in front of ye. Ye go because ye love what's behind ye. Yes, the guardian instinct, like all human instincts, is often twisted by sin. But the impulse to guard was always there. That's why Mordecai did what he did.'

15

JEREMIAH PUNCHED HIS friend in the shoulder. 'How's family life, Papa Morty?'

'Hadassah has an insane amount of energy.'

'I thought you hired part-time help.'

'I did. I'd be dead by now if I hadn't.'

'Regret it?'

'No. This is hard, but it still feels right. Plus, there are moments when I enjoy it.'

'Really?'

'Bits of it. Her tenth birthday is next week. We'll have a party—you should come.'

'Give me a minute,' Jeremiah said thoughtfully. 'I need to think of a reason why I can't.'

'Muttonhead.'

'Seriously, you going to survive this?'

'I'm not sure. I'm doing well at imports, but this parenting stuff is making me ask big questions.'

'Uh, oh. That sounds like the stuff Jews say before they—'

'—Emigrate to Israel? Yeah. It's been on my mind.'

'Why, exactly?'

'First, I'm wondering if the skills I've learned might be of value to the new government in Jerusalem. By the sound of things, they need help.'

'What's the other reason?'

'This city. Is it any place to raise a girl? You know how it is. Step outside the Jewish quarter, and it's nearly impossible to find a godly example of femininity. The city is full of culture, but it's also full of sin. Plus, the relatives in Israel would be a big help in raising Hadassah.'

'What's the matter, Morty? Dreading puberty already?'

'Don't go there.'

Mordecai contemplated moving to Israel with his cousin. But then his second promotion came. A timely word from the now semi-retired Joshua resulted in the city's Satrap offering him a director's position that would typically have been beyond the reach of his mere five years of experience. He was now head of Susa's import department and, though young, he worked hard and displayed natural gifting. Knowing that the job came with help from one of his heroes rekindled his childhood vision for service. *Heaven wants national Israel to re-emerge. But hasn't Heaven destined us to be a light to the nations?* he often mused.

Six years flew by, and Hadassah grew into a lovely and capable young woman. During this time, Xerxes returned defeated and designated the Empire's running to administrators while he drowned his depression in wine and women. Mordecai was one of many department heads that filled the management vacuum. His personal goals got pushed back as a result too.

'Are you single because you're so ugly?' Hadassah teased.

'I'm outrageously handsome. But I don't have time for dates!'

Hadassah proved intelligent enough to engage Mordecai in real dialogue. At times, the relationship began to feel something akin to a friendship—like what cousins who are close in age often enjoy.

She was now at the threshold of her fifteenth birthday and had become dangerously attractive. This unfortunate state of affairs meant that Mordecai was guarding her against an orc-army of suitors. The chubby nine-year-old with a crooked smile had blossomed—blossomed into a significant responsibility. Underneath his confident demeanour, it felt awkward. Many of the suitors were his age. One even worked in the citadel in an office nearby. But Mordecai, with the excuse of being busy, chose to pretend that her fifteenth birthday was still years away.

The Girl and the Guardian

16

HADASSAH BIT HER lip as she restrained the torrent of words inside of her. She grabbed a fig from the clay bowl on the table, separating her from her cousin and focused on the fruit as if it might magically channel her angst into constructive dialogue.

She took a deep breath. 'Hasn't Heaven wanted our people to return for decades now? Why would we disobey that?'

Mordecai recognised that the temperature of the conversation was higher than usual and attempted to diplomatise, as was his habit. He avoided arguments—especially with his cousin. 'I think we both agree that a person should do whatever they believe Heaven is calling them to do.'

Her cousin's response didn't help her control her pent-up emotions. She didn't want to pretend like everything was okay; not tonight. 'That doesn't answer my question. I'm asking: why we are not returning to Israel?'

Mordecai wanted to keep the peace, but the urge to defend himself before Hadassah's barrage of questions was growing. 'I honour Heaven with my work at the citadel,' he replied.

The Oliver Anderson Trilogy

'But how is it honouring Heaven to have a comfortable job in the citadel if Heaven has called us to return? Isn't that unfaithfulness?'

'That's not how I see it.' Mordecai didn't like conflict but felt pushed into it. An argument about politics and religion was suddenly upon him, and it was squashing the open-hearted discussion they both wanted to have.

'Is your career and the money more important than connecting with our family and national roots?! Is that why you prefer 'Mordecai' to your Hebrew name? Do your co-workers even know you're a Jew?'

Her words hurt. 'You think I'm ashamed of our people? Do you know who donated more money to Susa's Jewish widow's fund than anyone else last year?' he asked in cool defensiveness.

'How would the God of Israel take care of his widows if it weren't for palace money?' she asked sarcastically.

'Palace money builds our houses, schools—palace money even helped to build our synagogue.'

Hadassah realised her words were going too far and tried to reign them in 'I'm just confused. How can you serve a pagan king like Xerxes—a man who devours wine and women?'

'He's just doing what all kings do,' Mordecai said nonchalantly—but he regretted the words just after they left his mouth. He knew there was no moral justification for Xerxes' behaviour. He thought about how he might take back what he'd said, but it was too late.

Hadassah threw the fig into the bowl. 'Just doing what kings do?! Do you know how many girls he forces to screw him in that harem of his—or don't you care because you're a man? He probably thinks that's the only thing pretty girls are good for—screwing! How can you serve a tyrant-pig like that?!'

Her words were annoying him, but Mordecai still managed not to raise his voice. 'What about the eunuchs?' he asked.

Hadassah hated how cool Mordecai was in response. It seemed like he only did so to show how self-controlled he was compared to how out of control she felt. 'What about those freaks?'

'It's not like their genitals grew wings and flew away. The government butchers the penis and balls off 500 boys a year—forcing them into eunuch slavery.'

Hadassah shot him a glare, not even trying to hide the fire in her eyes. 'Is this supposed to make us girls feel better?!'

'You're the one who made it about gender. I'm merely pointing out that determining who has it worse isn't a simple business.'

The air was electric, hot, and laden with expletives. 'You think I'm simple and can't understand such big issues?' She gazed at him with her tongue pressed against her cheek in the contemptuous way girls do when they attempt to out-man you.

'Being a girl has nothing to do with it. I've trained you to be smarter than most Jewish boys your age. But now I'm worried that some teachers have filled your head with anti-Persian ideas. Heaven cares for all the nations, not just Israel.'

53

'Okay, so it's not that I'm a girl. You believe I can't think for myself—that someone has brainwashed me. Well, guess what Mr.Keeps-His-Cool, I'm not a nine-year-old girl anymore. I'm a Jewish woman who can think and fight for herself. I'm not a coward who's going to hide behind a name like "Esther". I'm a strong Jewish woman who's ready for marriage and adulthood!'

Mordecai rubbed his chin. 'I'll make a note of it,' he said casually.

'Obnoxious man!'

And with that, she turned and flew to her bedroom. The harsh and pointed words they said but didn't mean—and the helpful words they meant but didn't say—had kept them from the conversation they needed. They had sharpened their comments on the whetstone of anxiety instead of dressing their ears in understanding.

Mordecai sighed and stared into the espresso shaded discouragement in front of him. He wished his uncle Abihail was still alive to father his daughter. *Raise my cousin? Sure! How hard can it be?* He tidied up, then fell into bed with a giant serving of heaviness and a side dish of his cousin's scorn.

That would be the last they spoke for a long time.

The Girl and the Guardian

17

OLIVER WHISTLED UP at the kitchen ceiling. 'That Hadassah sure is feisty.'

'Aye. That lass could be a crazy broad when she got worked up.'

Oliver gave his grandfather a reproachful look. 'I think it's seen as impolite to call women "broads" nowadays, grandpa.'

'You don't say? Is it also impolite to call them crazy?'

Oliver laugh-choked on his coffee. 'Touché,' he said in a surrendered tone.

'Hadassah and Mordecai cared for each other—deeply so. They enjoyed each other's company and conversation. But, now that Hadassah was becoming an adult, social and political differences threatened disunity. That Hadassah was a proud nationalist—and Mordecai an overly-diplomatic servant of the Persian crown—didn't help.'

Oliver shook his head and sighed. 'Politics.'

They looked out at the surrounding deep green landscape. Grey clouds stretched from one end of the horizon to the other

The Oliver Anderson Trilogy

as the wind howled past the window. A typical day in the Highlands.

'Did grandma Anderson like this story?' Oliver asked.

'It was one of her favourites,'

'I wish I could've known her. She's so beautiful in your old pictures.'

'She was one of the loveliest lasses in our county.'

Oliver smiled impishly. 'Did she, like Hadassah, have an "unachievable backside"?'

William raised his voice. 'Careful how ye talk about yer grandmother, laddie!' But, after a pause, he broke out in a grin. 'Well, I suppose it was unachievable—unachievable to all except me!'

Oliver laughed. 'Grandpa Anderson's a silver fox!'

'Be grateful I was a charmer. Ye wouldn't be here if I weren't.'

'Cheers grandpa,' Oliver said as stretched out in his chair. 'Speaking of Hadassah, why do you think God, if he exists, gives more beauty to some than others?'

'God distributes beauty in a way that seems indiscriminate and, some might think, unfair. It is both spiritual and bodily, and we see it especially manifestin' in women. St. Paul wrote that "the woman is the glory of man". Women adorn humanity, spiritually and bodily, in a way that we men don't.'

'So God made 'em hot to make men happy?'

'Hot isn't the same as bonnie. God creates men and women, ultimately for himself. But women give somethin' to us men

The Girl and the Guardian

that we men can't give to each other. Femininity reflects God in a nourishin' and delightful way. Sin infuses beauty with challenges—both to the beholder and to the beheld. But ye need to remember that beauty isn't bad—though it can be used for bad. And feminine beauty in particular, well, that's like nuclear power: when ye use it properly, there is enormous potential for good. When ye misuse it, there's equal power for destruction.'

'Yes! Girls are like nukes! Hashtag, Grandad Wisdom.'

'Not sure what that means, but I'm glad ye approve. Now—'

'Back to the story?'

'Precisely.'

18

THE NEXT MORNING, Mordecai lumbered out of the house and turned to see the sun climb over the Zagros mountains and bathe Susa's white buildings in its morning gold. The mountain air ensured that the city wasn't too hot at dawn. By midday, however, the city would be baking.

Hadassah was still in her bedroom when he closed the door and began his walk to the citadel. He regretted not being able to apologise for his role in the argument the night before. *Oh well, I'll do it tonight.*

The workplace emitted a strange vibe that day, and he found himself scratching his head as whispers leaked from behind the doors of his superiors about something called 'the roundup'. He began looking for answers after the midday meal. He was dictating a purchase order to secretaries when the building rumbled. Dozens of soldiers galloped past the office, and everyone in the room looked to Mordecai for an explanation. He did not have one. That many soldiers usually meant violence. For a brief second, he feared for Hadassah. *No,* he reassured himself, *there's never violence of that type in the*

Jewish quarter. He was, however, frustrated enough to ask for an explanation from higher up, so he crossed the citadel to the office of Susa's Satrap. Typically, the secretary would be all a visitor saw. Mordecai, however, had ascended high enough to warrant a notice making its way back to the Satrap's desk. After a ten-minute wait, the office doors swung open. Mordecai entered.

The room had all the ornaments one might expect of a Persian ruler. Whoever had designed the room had undoubtedly wanted to impress—if not intimidate. The Satrap grinned from behind the finely carved table. 'Greetings, Mordecai! How is our youngest and most prodigious of administrators?'

Mordecai was put at ease by the Satrap's warm greeting and bowed. 'Your Greatness, I'm busy, but well.'

'You labour for the King. Good. How can we help you?'

'Your Greatness, I seek an explanation of today's events. Soldiers galloped from the citadel into the city. There are whispers of a "roundup", and I'm unable to reassure those who work under me. Are we bringing in a network of rebels or criminals?'

The Satrap plucked a grape from the silver bowl on his table and looked at Mordecai thoughtfully. 'You have nothing to fear. There is no big rebellion. No sedition.'

'I'm relieved to hear it. But what should I make of the soldiers?'

'Mordecai, my boy, you serve the Empire well, but the nature of this operation demands secrecy. Panic erupts easily, and we want to guard against that.' He swallowed the grape and sucked his teeth with epicurean relish. 'You see, the Emperor is in want of a new wife, and the magi have proposed a new method for selecting one—a strategy that the stars say will bring great blessing to the Empire.'

'His Majesty won't arrange a marriage with a royal princess in the traditional manner?'

'That's right. Remember how things with Vashti ended? She was a powerful princess. Our Emperor found her beautiful but rebellious. Between you and me, princesses and aristocrat daughters can make spoiled wives.'

'All of this makes sense Your Greatness, but what has this to do with the soldiers. Will they escort the new bride to the palace?'

The Satrap's grin widened. 'Escort her? Well, after a manner, I suppose. You see,' he lowered his voice, 'The King hasn't chosen the girl yet. He will hold a contest to determine who will be the Queen.'

'A contest?'

'I suppose it's fine to tell you now. The news will explode soon enough. As we speak, soldiers in Susa, Pasargadae, Persepolis, Anshan, Babylon, and in each of the cities of royal status throughout the Empire are rounding up that city's ten most beautiful maidens from non-aristocratic families. They chose these girls weeks ago, but we've waited for the right

The Girl and the Guardian

moment to snatch them all up. We escort them, as you say, back here, and then the Emperor chooses his Queen from among them.'

Hadassah.

'What a wise idea.' Fears scurried through Mordecai's mind like rats across a dirty floor. 'It's so deserving of our great Emperor. How, may I ask, will His Majesty select from among them?'

'How? How do you think? The eunuchs will beautify the girls with treatments and, when they are ready, each girl will have her night with the Emperor. The girl who pleases him the most will become the new Queen.'

Hadassah.

'He'll spend a night with every girl?'

'Yes, Mordecai. How else would he do it?'

'I, um, suppose most men would not be adequately sympathetic to the great challenges our glorious King is willing to undertake for the good of the Empire.'

'The King is noble in all he does.'

Mordecai forced a nod. 'Of course. And what, may I ask, will happen to the girls not chosen to be Queen? Will the palace return them?'

The Satrap coughed on his grape mid-swallow. 'Have you hit your head!? Returned? To their families? A man of your position in the service should know better. The palace never returns its girls. What if she were to one day marry, and her new husband said, "I sleep with the same woman the Emperor once did."

61

That would be a disgrace! I'll forget you asked such a question—but only this once.'

'Thank you. So that means the girls—'

'Yes, the other girls will live out their days in the royal harem.'

Hadassah!

'Thank you, Your Greatness. I have taken up enough of your time with my foolishness. I must hurry back to work.'

'Yes, I think that would be best, Mordecai. Get some rest.'

'Thank you, Your Greatness,' Mordecai said, getting up and hurrying out of the room. When he got out of the building, he started running. He did not stop until he reached his empty home.

The Girl and the Guardian

19

THE AIR SMELLED of cardamom, roses, and intrigue. That was one clue. There were more.

Hadassah wondered at the scope and splendour of the room. Its walls grew higher than trees and sunlight poured through its enormous windows. Mounted paintings captivated the beholder, giant pillows invited the weary to sleep, and waterfalls trickled down into sparkling pools. Dainty morsels filled golden platters and, after some initial hesitation, Hadassah found them to be the richest she'd ever tasted.

She assumed this was the palace or at least some other stately building nearby. Unlike her cousin, she rarely had the opportunity to pass through the gates and into the citadel. Ironically, the soldiers who would usually keep her out had now carried her in. Hadassah noted there were others. Nine other girls wandered about the room—all of them just as bewildered. Most were slow to engage in conversation as suspicion was a natural trait for those raised in Susa.

She rubbed her bruised shin. The wound wasn't from the soldiers—they had taken exceptional care with her. It had come

63

from tripping over the table when she attempted to simoultaneously throw a bowl of figs at them and run into her bedroom for her dagger. It didn't help that she was yelling 'Gentile dogs!' while performing this stunt.

Good job, klutz. Way to be classy.

Her mind returned to the mystery at hand. Were they suspected of crimes? Were they being recruited as help for another of Xerxes endless parties where she would be a cleaner or a food server?

One thing she noticed about the girls is that they were all stunning. She was used to being the prettiest girl in any room—*not a good habit,* she admitted. Mordecai had taught her not to base her confidence in appearance, but she still found it an easy thing to do. In her current company, those feelings of superiority vanished.

Lastly, it was apparent that someone was detaining them. Hadassah was the first among the ten girls to get irritated enough to seek answers. She approached the strangely dressed and beardless guards. *Probably foreigners,* she thought. She asked one of them matter-of-factly, 'Can you explain to me why we're here?'

He responded in an effeminate voice. 'Our boss will explain everything when he arrives. Please be patient.'

She tried again five minutes later, with more politeness, charm, and eyelashes—tools she had become adapt to using with men over the last year or so. Again, he told her to wait.

So far, so bad.

She tried a third time. She ditched her charm and bullied the guard. 'Do you know who my dad is?! He's a lead administrator in the civil service! He'll be furious when he finds out you are keeping me here with no explanation!' Hadassah rarely referred to Mordecai as her 'dad', but she thought it might carry more weight than 'cousin' in this instance. The guard looked uncomfortable in the face of her tirade, but he did not respond.

Threatening the guards with Mordecai's wrath turned her thoughts to him. *Where is he?* She knew her cousin had connections and would be on his way to rescue her out of this crazy situation. The argument from the night before flashed through her mind. No point thinking about that now. *When Mordecai gets me out, I'll apologise for my harsh words.*

***

'Hadassah! Hadassah!' Mordecai screamed as he ran through the house and into her bedroom. She wasn't there. *Heaven, no!* He spun around and rushed back to the street, looking it up and down. 'Hadassah! Hadassah!' Mordecai fought to breathe after his long sprint and the horror of the unthinkable. His head spun irrationally in every possible direction, desperate to see her. 'Hadassah!'

Men and women came out to the street and surrounded their hysterical neighbour. 'Have you seen her!' he pleaded as they approached. Two ladies reported that five soldiers had come and that a war had erupted inside Mordecai's house before they came back out carrying Hadassah. They had forcibly mounted her on a horse and ridden away.

They tried to reassure him. 'Surely, it's a mistake!', 'Hadassah couldn't have done anything criminal!', 'They will realise their error and bring her back soon!'—all positive assertions to make sense of why soldiers had taken the neighbourhood darling.

But Mordecai knew the truth. No one would bring her back—not that night, not the next day, not ever. She was gone. Speechless, Mordecai waved his neighbours away and turned towards the house. He needed a minute to be alone. He needed to think.

He squashed a fig beneath his sandal as he entered. Others lay scattered across the floor, mixed with clay shards. A previously organised pile of clothes had erupted in all directions. *There's no way she'd go without a fight.* He walked into her room and checked underneath her bed—her dagger was still there. *Not that it would've done much good against a group of armed soldiers.*

He walked back into the centre room, picked up a chair, and sat down between a sock and his sanity. He reviewed what had happened, hoping he might discover a way out. Maybe they'd return some of the girls. Could it be a post-argument nightmare that he'd soon wake-up from?

As the minutes—or was it hours?—passed, reality fell on him. Emotions flooded in. Though he worked near the palace, he realised it would be impossible to ever see her. As part of the

The Girl and the Guardian

King's harem, they'd keep her in a different part of the castle, under the watch of guards.

An avalanche of guilt collapsed on his shoulders. The synagogue elders had entrusted him to be Hadassah's guardian. He'd failed. *If only I'd given her in marriage or moved to Israel! If only I'd done other than I did—this wouldn't have happened!*

The self-pity spun his soul downward like water being sucked through a drain and into the sewers. Darkness set in. Will Hadassah ever know happiness? Heaven, forgive me. Be with her now. Mordecai knew an abrupt goodbye with someone who owned as much of his heart's real-estate as Hadassah did was enough to make a man die a little. Or a lot. He needed help. He stood, spat profanities all over the floor, and stumbled out towards Jeremiah's.

20

'MENTAL HOW THEY kidnapped her! Will Mordecai destroy half of Susa to get her back like Liam Neeson in Taken?'

'I'm afraid Mordecai, strong as he may be, has neither the guns nor the CIA trainin' to pull that off.'

'But kidnapping a girl is something to fight about—like that book by the Greek guy in Troy when Helen gets taken, and the two armies do battle till they make that big horse thing.'

'Yes, I'm familiar with the work by Homer.'

'Homer, yes. But you get the point. It's an act of war!'

'Well, the Bible would agree with ye. It says there's a spiritual war happenin' around the whole issue of beauty—and there has been since evil first entered humanity.'

'What's a spiritual war look like?'

'Counterfeit beauties that come straight from ol' Black Donald.'

'Huh?'

'Sorry, my London laddie, that's "the Devil" in these parts. He prances around as an angel of light. He separates Beauty from Truth and Goodness. These counterfeit beauties uglify the souls of those who consume them. Vanity, pornography, seduction, immorality, deceptive advertising, immodesty—all ways that ol' Black Donald seeks to destroy us.'

'They aren't merely bad habits?'

'Believers see them as acts of spiritual war.'

Oliver rubbed his chin and looked up. 'Maybe that's what I need—a script set in the middle of battle or war. I could create a plot around a small group of soldiers in the trenches.'

'Ye can place a good story anywhere, and it works. War's a helpful settin' for stories that remind us about the fragility of life and humanity's potential ugliness. But, before ye decide on yer settin', ye need a story.'

'Yes, I do. And if I'm aiming for a beautiful story, maybe the trenches aren't the best setting.'

'Why'd ye say that?'

'Because the trenches of World War One are one of the ugliest places imaginable. I know you know that.'

'Aye, I'm well aware. But that doesn't mean you can't tell a beautiful story in it.'

'It'd be hard, though. Right?'

'We often find the most beautiful things amidst the ugliest circumstances.'

'Is that true of the spiritual war you were talking about?'

William nodded his head solemnly. 'It's truer there than anywhere else.'

'How does one win a spiritual war—a war against the devil and counterfeit beauty? I get that you probably don't mean a

69

crusade or jihad. You're not talking about suicide bombers. When you say "spiritual war," I think of things used to fight vampires—garlic, crucifixes, and such.'

'Believers win their spiritual battles by the power of the Beautiful Ugly.'

'The Beautiful Ugly?'

'Aye. The Jews in Esther's day were lookin' forward to when the Messiah would come. He would help set all these things right. Orthodox Jews are still waiting for a Messiah—which is where Christians and believin' Jews differ. As a Christian, I believe the Messiah has already come and that he's won the decisive battle.'

'Sounds naïve. The world's still filled with problems related to beauty.'

'Oh, no doubt about it. From the battle over Helen, as ye mentioned, to the Nazi quest for the perfected Aryan race, to today's eatin' disorders and pornography addictions—we've had a violently dysfunctional relationship to beauty.'

'Then how can you say that some Messiah has won a decisive battle?'

'You've heard the sayin' "Don't judge a book by its cover", haven't ye?'

'Everybody has.'

'Do ye do it? Does everyone who's heard that sayin' obey it?'

'No, I guess we don't. We still judge by appearances,' Oliver confessed.

'Christians believe that the pow'r to experience change and live free from beauty dysfunction is available.'

'How?'

'Jesus is God's eternal word. He had an eternal beauty—far greater than Hadassah. His brighter-than-the-sun beauty was the centre of Heaven. And what d'ya think he did with it?'

'I don't know.'

'He gave it all away. He died the most horrid of deaths. He became the Beautiful Ugly.'

'Why'd he do that?'

'So that ye and I might have the only beauty that matters.'

'How's that work?'

'The Beautiful Ugly is the Tree where he died—where he exchanges his radiance for our repulsiveness. If the Tree is ugly, it's our ugliness up there. His beauty comes to us. The Tree is a wrecking ball that shatters this world's ideas about beauty to their foundations.'

'That's intense. I think maybe we should—'

'Aye. As ye wish.'

21

On the opposite side of the city, a father and son entered an enormous room humming with activity. 'And this is where the magic happens,' the father said proudly.

The young man's mouth dropped open. His older brothers had responded the same way in years previous. 'The noise! It sounds like a hive of bees. How does it all work?'

His father, Haman, pointed with his hand. 'You see the men working on those tables, Aridai? They're our traditional scribes. They press letters into the clay tablets and cylinders with reeds. They write the messages I give them in Persian as well as whatever language the country that it is sent to speaks.'

'What about those men in the far corner?'

'Ah, I'm glad you noticed them. This has been a reform of my own since taking over. Those men are writing the same messages, but they're doing so on something called a scroll. It was a risky decision, as we stole this technology from the Greeks. Some low-level workers protested the idea. They really tried to fight me over it. But the scrolls are now paying off. They'll be the future of all our communications.'

72

'Have the workers who complained about your decision changed their minds?'

'No, of course not.'

'No? Why not?'

'They're dead. I had soldiers shoot them through with arrows as a public display. An imperial minister should never tolerate rebellion for the lowest ranks. Understand?'

'Yes, father.'

'A leader must be quick to punish offences lest they spread.'

Aridai smiled at his father—a man who held the life and death of others in his hand. 'What do you tell these scribes to write? Are they the King's words?'

'Xerxes approves all the messages. They are, after all, in his name. It's the responsibility of Imperial Communications to ensure they go out effectively to all the provinces. Some messages might seem boring to you, but we perform a vital role: we hold the Empire together by making sure everyone hears the same story.'

'What story?'

'That the Persian Empire brings relief from the injustices of lesser kingdoms. The light of liberation pushes back the darkness of oppression through the majestic leadership of King Xerxes and the Achaemenid dynasty.'

'Is it a true story?'

'King Xerxes loves the truth. He wouldn't proclaim it to the world if he didn't believe it.'

'Do you believe it's true?'

'What is truth, son?'

Aridai thought for a moment. 'I'm not sure how to say it. But I know the truth when I feel it. At least, I think I do.'

'The truth is that we're Amalekites. And not merely Amalekites, we're Agags—descendants from Amalekite kings. Yes, your mother is a Persian aristocrat, and a lovely one at that. But always remember, you also have royal blood in your veins. You have the inner power to change this world and make it a better place.'

Aridai gazed at his father in admiration. 'I wish we were still kings.'

'So do I son. Perhaps, one day—but it isn't wise to talk like this at the citadel. For now, we say that it is a great honour to be a royal servant and councillor in the world's most powerful Empire.'

'Was it difficult to become one of the King's councillors as a foreigner?'

'Working my way up was hard. The Persian Empire treats foreigners with greater equality than previous empires. Still, I had to fight. Many Persians are prejudiced, even if they rarely admit it. It was a tall ladder to climb going from the son of a fruit merchant to an imperial councillor. Plus, who's to say I've stopped climbing?'

'If we were Agags, why did grandpa sell fruit?'

Haman's jaw tightened. Should he tell his son, or not? He knew his wife didn't share the feelings he had towards the Amalekite's historical enemies, and she disapproved of him imparting those feelings to their children. With a furrowed brow, he stared into his son's eyes. 'It was a great injustice—a wicked nation is responsible for it.'

'Which nation?'

Haman decided he wouldn't hold the truth from his son. 'Israel. The Jews. They've been our enemies for centuries. We should've eliminated them then when they were only a tribe wandering in the wilderness. Later, under the leadership of the king Saul, Israel almost wiped us out. They're why we're no longer kings.'

'But our family survived.'

'Yes, but without our glory. That Susa even has a Jewish quarter is sickening. That Cyrus reestablished Israel after Babylon had destroyed it, is a tragedy. But we must be careful about how we speak. Your mother doesn't like it. Plus, one must be careful about ascribing a mistake to even a dead Persian king.'

Aridai nodded. 'I understand.'

22

OLIVER OPENED HIS EYES 'That guy Haman has issues. Talk about anti-semitism!'

'It'd surprise you how popular, though subtle, it still is. There's no shortage of people callin' for the death of Isreal in both mosques and academic halls the world over.'

'Haman seems so evil. Like a Nazi from the ancient world.'

'Haman was a wretched but sophisticated man. We'd be mistaken to think such men and such evil only exists in stories from long ago or for a moment during the Second World War.'

'He makes my skin crawl,' Oliver said, taking another sip of coffee.

'The taste seems to be growing on you. Want another?'

'Soon, perhaps. You know, I'm thinking about what you said earlier.'

William grinned. 'A welcome change.'

'Ouch. I do listen, you know. I mean what you said about there being a difference between hot and beautiful, or "bonnie".'

'Well done. I'll make Scotsman of ye yet.'

The Girl and the Guardian

'Good luck with that. But I think I understand your point. I can imagine a beautiful woman without thinking about sex. But when I imagine a hot girl, sex hovers close by. I could look at female relatives and think they're beautiful, but I'd never think they're hot.'

'Glad to hear my grandson's not a pervert.'

'Cheers. But doesn't the Bible tell women to cover up? You talk about feminine beauty, but I've always had the impression that Christian women should dress, I dunno, prudishly.'

'St. Paul called Christian women to be modest in his letter to a pastor named Timothy.'

Oliver shook his head in disapproval. 'What's the point of making women beautiful if you then command them to cover it all up?'

'Modesty helps us avoid beauty's pitfalls. In this context, St. Paul was speaking to women of a certain socio-economic level about adornin' themselves using gold and pearls. Next to them were women of a lower class who couldn't afford such things. Ye see, an immodest person draws attention to themselves to assert superiority. Paul doesn't want women doin' this—to dress proudly like Vashti did. Ye understand his point? It can be divisive.'

'Makes sense, I suppose. I've seen plenty of girls proudly flaunt their looks and bodies about.'

'I bet ye have.'

Oliver grinned. 'Well, I'm not saying that it's all bad.'

'Men can be immodest too—but in different ways. Another reason the Bible calls us to modesty is that exaltin' our beauty over others blinds us to our inner ugliness. Dark hearts can have a pretty face, and beautiful hearts can hide inside a plain appearance.'

'Yeah, I've known girls like that too: beautiful, but nasty!'

'Well, speakin' of beauty's pits, let's see how Hadassah is doing in hers.'

The Girl and the Guardian

23

THE HOURS CRAWLED slowly by. At sunset, another oddly dressed man, also beardless, came through the doors. He seemed, based on the deference the guards viewed him with, to be a man of authority. He raised his hands and said with a loud voice, 'Welcome ladies. My name is Hegai, and I'm in charge here.'

Like the guards, he was beardless and his voice high. Hadassah was not used to being around beardless men and found their features to be amusingly kitten-like. Hegai, aka Mr.In-Charge, continued his speech. 'I realise you must have many questions. Unfortunately, I am not able to answer them all right now as not all of you are here yet. Once we've gathered everyone, I'll explain more. Please eat and rest. There is no need to fear. We'll treat you with the utmost care. I only ask for your patience.' Hadassah raised her hand, eager to ask a question. Hegai, however, wasn't taking questions. He turned and left.

Well, they aren't treating us like criminals. She wondered what Hegai had meant by 'once we've gathered everyone'. While musing, she helped herself to another pastry. Though

79

Mordecai provided well for them, she had never tasted such refined food. *I want this pastry to be a man so I can drag him to the synagogue and marry him.* As she finished that one, resisting the temptation to reach for yet a third, she sensed someone standing beside her. She turned and looked into the face of a girl with big and fearful eyes.

'Hello.'

'Hello.'

'D—do you know why we're here?'

'I'm afraid I don't,' Hadassah confessed.

'Oh. I'm sorry. It's only... I have no idea what's going on, and it's been so long n, now' she stuttered then began to sob.

Hadassah embraced the stranger and then looked her in the eyes. 'I'm afraid no one does. But I trust we'll get more answers tomorrow.'

The girl nodded. 'My name is Azar, what's yours.'

'It's Had—,' she paused. 'Esther. My name is Esther.'

The girl smiled. 'It's nice to meet you.'

Esther found a few pillows, a luxurious silk sheet, and attempted to fall asleep—a feat she accomplished with minimal success. Whenever she would fall asleep, anxiety would descend like a troll sent to rob her of calm. She would awake with a start and look around to see the other girls sleeping. Her mind somersaulted with emotions. Anger from being kept against her consent. Hope in Mordecai finding her. Fear in the uncertainty of what would happen. Weakness in not being able to change her circumstances. And regret over her words such as

The Girl and the Guardian

'obnoxious man' which she knew had cut deep into her cousin's heart.

Then, she felt an urge welling up inside her that she hadn't felt in some time. She felt the need to call out to the God of her people. Prayer was not uncommon in her house. Mordecai prayed, had taught her to pray, and she recited prayers at school. But this urge was different. She didn't need to recite prayers. She needed to pray—an activity that, when correctly done, requires humility. There, in that strange and beautiful place, under unknown circumstances and far from Mordecai, she began to call upon the true King of Israel with tears. There, in that golden cage, the Psalms of David that she had memorised made the journey from head to heart.

Over the last year, she had given her attention to Israel as Heaven's nation. Now she was thinking about the One who sat on Heaven's throne. Here, far from Mordecai, and even farther from the Holy Land—in the centre of pagan power and corruption—the world's true King knew who she was and what she was going through. At that moment, she cared little for politics and began to speak by faith in her vulnerability to the One she knew was the Guardian of the orphans and the needy. And, in sharing her heart with Him, she fell asleep.

***

The next morning, ten more girls arrived. Like the ones already present, they were all Hadassah's age and all stunningly beautiful. But these girls came from Babylon. Two hours later, another ten girls arrived from yet a different city. Then an hour later, another ten.

Soon the room was filled with various skin colours and the sound of various languages. Girls from throughout the Empire began to relax, enjoy food and wine, and introduce themselves. Hadassah also began to chat with Azar and the other girls and soon found herself having a good time.

It was not until late afternoon when the final group of girls arrived that the coin dropped. Someone exclaimed that the room was beautiful enough to be a royal harem. The other girls, half silly with too much wine, laughed. But not Hadassah. Her heart raced as a new thought trickled into her mind.

How could I have been so dumb! Not having been in the citadel before, she had never seen a eunuch up close. But now it made sense. No wonder the guards seem so effeminate! But she did not have the heart space to pity them. Her stomach knotted at the sight of the other beautiful girls, and she began to shake. 'No!' she rebuked the universe for its unfairness. 'The King has enough girls!'

Her head spun with the realisation that, if she was correct, not even Mordecai could rescue her now. *No! Control yourself! You don't know the whole story yet!* She collapsed back onto a pillow like a marionette with its strings cut, buried her face in her knees, and wept.

When many young women were gathered in Susa
the citadel in the custody of Hegai,
Esther also was taken into the king's palace
and put in custody of Hegai, who had charge of the women.
-Esther 2.8

83

The Oliver Anderson Trilogy

24

'LIKE A PUNCH to the throat.'

'What's that?'

Oliver sat down in his chair, having just made another mug of coffee. 'What it would be like, as a girl, to realise men trafficked you, and that there is no escape? It's hard to imagine a darker place.'

'This sex contest only exists because the King is a lust monkey whose pleasure island is never big enough to satisfy him. Not that we should self-righteously condemn him. Based on web traffic, Xerxes is only doing what most men would do if ye made 'em Emperor.'

'You can't compare what Xerxes did to porn. No one gets hurt in porn.'

'Isn't that naïve?'

'Okay, yes, maybe some people do get hurt. But not everyone. Is this where you condemn those who think differently about sex and gender?' Oliver asked, making it sound like an accusation more than a genuine question. 'Christians are

The Girl and the Guardian

so backward on this. They say such rubbish things about human sexuality.'

William smiled calmly and reached for his pipe on the counter next to the table. He pulled a lighter from his trousers, lit it, and took a couple of puffs before responding. 'Most Christians say nothin' about it, ye see. They fear that people will condemn them for wrong-think.'

'And rightfully so! I mean, who are they to judge what other people do? All forms of sex are equally beautiful if you're open-minded.'

'And that attitude is why most believers find expressin' their view of sexuality about as challengin' as playing Jenga on a waterbed with an overweight five-year-old.'

'Wow. Now you're fat-shaming.'

'That's a thing?'

Oliver decided educating his grandfather on the evil of fat jokes would be a distraction to the subject at hand. 'We live in the 21st Century, where people celebrate all forms of sexuality. Sexual beauty is in the eye of the beholder. Who are we to judge?'

William paused for a moment. 'Well, what do ye think? Is Xerxes' form of sexuality beautiful?'

'Well, no. His practices are monstrous.'

'Who are ye to judge him? I imagine that from Xerxes' perspective, the scenery may not be so bad.'

'That's different. Xerxes is pulling in all these girls against their will. It's hardly consensual.'

William took a long puff and asked, 'So, what you're sayin' is that if sex is consensual, then the sky's the limit for what people should do?'

Oliver had enoyed his grandfather's story up to this point, but he was certain that the old man would have nothing insightful to say on this subject. 'I simply think your Christian ideas about sex are dull and dated.'

'So ye think Christians are a bit sheltered because they haven't bought a sex robot yet?'

'If that's what someone enjoys, why should we judge them? We need to get with it.'

'Get with it? You mean bowin' down to society's sophisticated-soundin' insanity?'

'Insanity?!' Oliver was clearly irritated. 'It means that, though you might like sex between a man and a woman in marriage, your neighbour might have different tastes! What's wrong with that? Saying that your way is better is ignorant!'

William grinned and exhaled a smoke ring. 'Are ye suggestin' I need to be more sophisticated in my sexual views so that I can be acceptable?'

'It's not like that. Look, maybe I should send you a Youtube link that explains this better.'

'"Youtube"? What's that? Londoner slang for masturbation?'

Oliver couldn't help but laugh, breaking the building sense of tension he'd felt. 'No, gran—okay. Sorry, I got heated and said too much. I want to hear you out on this because there are so many stereotypes of what Christians believe. Start again. I'll listen better.'

'Glad to hear it, laddie. For orthodox Jews and Christians, it's simple. We believe that God has spoken—to the Jews through Moses and the Prophets. And, for Christians, they believe in Moses and the Prophets, but they also believe that Jesus is the promised Messiah. Despite that difference, ye see, there's agreement between the Hebrew Scriptures and the New Testament on sex and marriage. If God speaks, ye trust he knows what he's talkin' about.'

'Fair enough. But don't you want to understand "why" God gives that rule? Why would he teach that?'

'Ye take God at his word, even when ye don't understand— much like a young child should do what their parent says even when they don't understand a rule. But I do think we can comprehend God's design for this on this—part of the way, at least.'

'How?'

'Nowadays we say ridiculous things about our sexual organs that ye would never say about yer other organs. We tell ourselves that it's fine to rub our genitals against anyone or anythin'—so long as it's consensual, as ye pointed out. It's fascinatin' how this term "consensual" has become like a magic wand that ye wave over any sexual experience to make it morally acceptable.

'Well, if two people agree to it, how can it be wrong?'

'Since yer making up the rules, why stop at two?'

'Fair enough. If a group agrees, how can it be wrong?'

'If that's the case, ye can't speak of any higher purpose to sex. Ye emphasise the warmth and pleasure it gives. But God designed our world with meanin'—and this meanin' stretches even to yer sexuality.'

Oliver took a sip of his still scolding hot coffee. 'Meaning? I can't even write a script with meaning. My sex life, not that I have much of one, doesn't have any purpose beyond having fun for a moment.'

William nodded and took another puff. He appreciated his grandson's openness. 'Imagine talkin' about yer digestive organs in this way. Yer digestive organs have a purpose. There's such a thing as good and bad eatin'. Should ye swallow chocolate flavoured motor oil as long as it gives yer tongue nice feels? What about yer respiratory system? Are there things yer lungs should not breathe? What if someone said 'Well, ye might use yer lungs to give oxygen to your blood, but I don't feel drawn to that. My lungs like to sniff paint'? What if someone tattooed their eyes for decorative effect, but it caused them blindness? Does this go against the organ's purpose?'

'Of course.'

'As with these other organs, the meanin' of yer sexual organs must be about more than yer feelings. After all, ye can eat yerself and sniff yerself to an early death all while enjoyin' it, right? For our reproductive systems, we make an odd exception to this. We create slogans that proclaim sexual experience as anythin' ye like. They sound true but mean little. If sex is merely anythin' that makes yer willy excited or yer mood happy, then it becomes nothin' more than scratchin' a part of ye that itches.'

'Can't I have sex for the fun of it or to feel a sense of affection with someone?'

'Most people today do exactly that. What I'm tryin' to say is that, like with any other body part, when pleasure becomes yer main guiding principle, sex becomes hollow. Christians believe that sex should be both pleasurable and meaningful.'

Oliver tilted his head and shrugged his shoulders. 'Okay, I'll admit that our whole hook-up culture does make sex seem pretty shallow. But does this mean that because our sexual organs are part of our reproductive system, their only purpose is to create offspring?'

'Biologically speakin', aye. Yer genitals are there to make wee bairns.'

'Sex is for babies? You're really going to argue for that?'

'I know that idea makes cool kids stop pettin' their unicorns and act appalled. But we can't shame biology. True sex is God's design. He wove the joy and intimacy of sexual union together with the ability to reproduce.'

'So Christians believe that sex is for children and intimacy?'

'Sex creates new life by bringin' a husband and wife together in a strong union. That bond prepares them to be a mother and father that create and raise healthy wee bairns. Hormones, released durin' sex, cement ye together with yer wife—emotionally speakin'. Sex creates a unity of gender opposites to create a new life. Now that's somethin' worth celebrating, isn't it?'

'Yes. The ability to bring a new life into this world is amazing.'

'Aye. And ye know this intuitively. Why only three weeks ago, a young couple from my church invited me over their house for a sex party.'

Oliver chocked on a sip of his coffee. 'Wait. What?! You got invited where?'

'A sex party,' William explained. 'It's a new thing young couples are doing.'

'What exactly are we talking about?'

'It's new to me, but I figured ye'd know about it. It's when a couple announces whether the sex of the baby is male or female.'

Oliver sighed. 'Gender reveal. It's called a "gender reveal", grandpa.'

'Oh, aye. That's it.'

'It's important to get that one right when you fill out the card.'

William's eyebrows lifted. 'I need to bring a card?'

'Don't worry about it. It's not essential.'

'Anyway, my point is, the ability to bring this new baby girl or boy into the world is why God gave ye yer junk. That an untin' ye to yer woman.'

'So you think God gave us sex for these two purposes?'

'Aye. In sex, ye reinforce with yer body what we say with yer life. At a weddin', the man and the woman give themselves fully to each other. They pledge their whole lives to each other. Physically and emotionally, ye receive from the other what yer not. The feminine receives the masculine, and the masculine receives the feminine.'

Oliver nodded. 'I see why believers see such depth and meaning to doing it this way.'

'Yer grandmother and I found that the beauty of sex continued throughout our marriage. Once we had children, sex renewed the commitment we made to each other and created a lovely environment where our wee bairns could grow up.'

'I'm not wild on thinking about my grandparent's sex lives, but I see what you mean. Your beliefs gave sex a deep sense of purpose. But why does that mean we need to be cruel to those who disagree?'

'Cruel? Who said anythin' about being cruel?'

'But if you don't affirm other people's sexual practices, isn't that mean and intolerant?'

'Is it?'

'I think so.'

'There's be a popular notion floatin' about, particularly with young people, that if ye disagree with them on an important issue like sex, ye must hate them. That's nonsense. I believe sex is best according to God's design of one man and one woman for one lifetime. But I'm not cruel to those with a different opinion—and hopefully they won't be cruel to me.'

'Is it that simple?' Oliver asked sceptically.

'I don't see why not.'

'Okay. But what if someone says that you're painting too rosy a picture of marital sex? Not all married people, even Christians, have smoking hot sex lives.'

'Oh, Aye. But the problem doesn't lay in sex's design. We're fallen creatures. Jealousy, manipulation, abuse, hormonal imbalances, boredom, sickness, and adultery—they all twist sex from its relational purpose.'

'What do you mean by "relational purpose"?'

'Yer reproductive system is unique. Ye can digest food, breathe, and watch a sunset—all by yerself. But, to reproduce, ye must be in union with a woman. Men and women need each other to reproduce and healthily raise children.'

'I will admit that I'm thankful I grew up with a mum and a dad who stayed together. The thought of them divorcing or committing adultery isn't pleasant.'

'The children of these marriages receive both masculine and feminine input in ways that cause their emotional development to flourish. But, by contrast, adultery, pornography, harems, etc—they only ever have a twisted beauty at best and usually aren't ideal for children's development.'

'But adultery, pornography, and other types of sex are normal nowadays. People love it.'

'Aye. Sex like that may briefly brighten. But it casts a long shadow. We humans are skilled at doing what's bad for us. With all the celebratin' and noise about every and any type of sexual

The Girl and the Guardian

activity, few voices give ye warnin' about the infections, mental health, depression, divorce, and broken hearts that come with it. The parades conveniently forget to mention those mornin'-after side effects. Consumin' junk sex in our society is as easy as junk food. It's not only Xerxes. We're a society of lust monkeys.'

'Okay, grandpa. Thanks for sharing your perspective. It's different than what I usually hear in London.'

'Anytime. Back to the story?'

'Please.'

25

HADASSAH WIPED THE teardrops from her cheeks and gathered with the other girls around Hegai to hear what he had to say.

'Ladies!' The kitten-faced man cleared his throat to project his high-pitched voice. 'You are all finally here. I understand that the last day and a half traumatised some of you, but I don't want any of you to be afraid.'

Hadassah couldn't keep it in. 'That's not easy when we don't know what's going on!'

'I'm here to explain. Please calm down, sweetheart.'

She fought to keep her mouth shut as comebacks raced through her mind. *'Sweetheart'? 'Calm down'? Send me home you effeminate lizard! I'm Jewish! I don't belong here!*

Hegai continued his speech. 'If you have not figured it out already, you are in the King's harem.' The announcement electrified the room with panic as many of the girls had not yet understood the situation. 'Please, ladies, give me your attention. Ladies!' Hegai yelled, but lost control of the room.

The Girl and the Guardian

Hadassah sat back down on the pillow with disdain for everything and everyone in that room. *This is why we belong in Israel!* She watched as some girls started weeping and others began to walk towards doors to see if they could open them. The eunuch guards quivered with uncertainty as they tried to corral the seething mob of lovely femininity.

Then, something strange happened. Hadassah looked up at Hegai, the eunuch that she had been loathing. Desperation flashed from his eyes. Raising his squeaky voice to its height, he was unable to regain control. It was pitiful. And the pitifulness of his face shot through her hard heart like an arrow. The impact was almost as physical as it was emotional. Her mind tried telling her that this gentile deserved whatever he got. But her heart wouldn't listen.

The poor man.

Not one to do nothing, Hadassah knew she needed to act on what she felt. She remembered an old trick that Mordecai had taught her. She placed both hands up to mouth and released an enormous whistle that echoed off the ornate walls. The room fell quiet. With all eyes on her, she mustered an inner boldness to speak. 'Thank you, sir.' The room quieted at Hadassah's firm and clear voice. 'You have more to tell us, and we will listen. I'm sure you'll answer many of our questions if we give you our attention. Right girls?'

Hegai shot her a look of surprised gratitude. 'Thank you. Well, for starters, I'm not a "sir". I'm a eunuch, and I'm here to explain that we've chosen you all to be part of a grand contest.'

Whispers trickled through the room, but Hegai raised his voice again and managed to keep control. He managed to explain the contest and its rules without the room re-exploding into chaos. He finished by saying, 'I know that this news affects you in different ways. But I urge you to see how glorious this is. You will never want for food or drink again. We will give you silk clothes, the best meals, and luxurious accommodation. You will get to serve the King of kings, and one of you will be lucky enough to become Empress. You have tonight to calm yourselves and realise what a blessing this is. Tomorrow, six months of beauty treatments begin.'

Never before had a man fled so eagerly from a room bursting with so many beautiful young women. Hadassah pondered what had just happened while the rest chattered furiously. Her boldness had surprised her—the way she had taken control of the room. But she was even more surprised at the way Hegai's anxious expression had so moved her. With her increasing nationalism, Mordecai had often told her that Heaven loved people of all nations—but to no avail. Somehow that one look brought all those little, fatherly sermons to life.

She wondered where Heaven was in the midst of this craziness. How does being kidnapped square with Heaven's goodness?

26

'I GUESS IT was hard to be a beautiful girl in ancient Persia.'

'Yer right. Attention to physical appearance consumed the Persians. Every nobleman kept a make-up artist with him at all times, and fake beards and moustaches were a must-have item. Everyone competed to have the best possible image.'

'The men had full-time make-up artists?'

'Is yer polished social media world all that different? From profile pics to pornography to eatin' disorders to advertisin'— we see people chasin' after eye-catchin' images, don't we?'

'We've got issues, yeah.'

'Beauty isn't bad. God made it. We are his 'sub-creators'—to borrow a term from Mr.Tolkien. He wants us to beautify our world. That's why ye want yer script to be beautiful, like a musician wants her music to sound lovely or a mechanic wants his car to look good. Sin is why ye have so much difficulty with beauty.'

'Does sin mean we should avoid beauty?'

'Not at all! Enjoy it—but don't let it master ye. Beauty can be our delightful little sister, or it can be our dark and cruel slave-master. Believers trust that God will make all these crooked lines straight and make our relationship to beauty function properly before the end of all things.'

'Assuming such a future is real, what should we do in the meantime?'

'For now, whenever ye see a mountain, a bonnie lass, or a shootin' star, let delight come alive! In such moments, somethin' is callin' ye home.'

'Food for thought, grandpa. Any chance we would get back to what's happening in the harem?'

'Oh, it's getting' crazy with the lasses. Talk about the competition!'

'I guess competing over a perfect image would be a big part of what that contest was all about. Go ahead, continue.'

'Aye, alright. Turn yer face off and listen.'

27

MORDECAI PLACED HIS wine cup on the table and looked at Hadassah. She tore a piece of bread, using it to pick up some roasted lamb, oblivious to the clearing throat sound that fathers make when they want attention.

'Hadassah.'

'Yeah?'

'You're about to turn fourteen.'

'Yes, I know.'

'Fourteen is a big year for a beautiful girl. Are you ready?'

'Are you about to give a dad talk? Cause you're not brilliant at it.'

'I'm the closet thing you have to a parent. I'd rather say too much than too little.'

'Okay then. I'm listening.'

Give thanks for your appearance Hadassah, but wear it wisely.
Extend the same respect to plain girls as you do to the gorgeous.
Don't compare your beauty with theirs or else you'll become

bitter or vain—for there will always be girls of either greater or lesser beauty than yourself.

Be confident, but not loud or aggressive. Let your strength be subtle: slow to speak and quick to listen. Don't judge harshly, for even the despicable have a story to tell.

Be kind to all of Heaven's creation, both Jews and Persians, for this world's mean streets need people who are not themselves mean.

Mordecai's dinnertime lessons echoed through Esther's dreams—softening her heart and guiding her mind. While the harem schooled her in the best beauty and sexual techniques in Persia, Mordecai's lessons kept her rooted. Esther clung to the memories of her mentor's words and used his instruction to navigate her strange new world. She only wished she had paid better attention.

She needed navigation. Relational pitfalls were everywhere, and the girls lost themselves in the ugliest of competitions.

'My makeup is more seductive.'

'My boobs are perkier.'

'My leather knots are tighter.'

'You all aren't nearly flexible enough to do this!'

Esther's eyes rolled. 'We don't have to kill each other over this.'

'Don't pretend you don't want to win—Miss Perfect Figure.'

Such comments only enraged Esther. 'We all want to win! But we don't have to become estrogenic nightmares in the process!'

'So that's what you think of us!'

In addition to beauty products and designers, Hegai allowed the girls metaphysical support. Some of the magi were eunuchs, and the King had instructed those who were to attend to the girls. Some contestants used magi to call upon Persian spirits to enhance their sexuality with magic spells.

The girls ridiculed the eunuch guards when they were annoyed. 'Nutless, hairless monkeys! They herd us around from beauty treatment to beauty treatment like we're sheep. They never even speak to us.'

'They're not that bad,' Esther countered.

'I'm glad you like them, Esther. Since the King will be picking me, these eunuchs are the closest thing to a real man you're ever going to see.'

Esther, still felt ashamed when she remembered her last words spoken to Mordecai. Those words, shouted in political arrogance, were a stain on the inside of her that she couldn't scrub off. That memory made left her with a weight of self-disgust and made her painfully aware that she didn't have the right to look down on anyone, even a Persian eunuch. This humility was out of place among the Queen trainees. It won her some enemies as well as some allies. But the most unexpected relationship it earned her was with Hegai.

'Thank you for all you do for us, Hegai. I know we're not the easiest bunch to work with.'

Hegai didn't expect kind comments from concubines. 'I don't know if you'll win the Queenship, but you've won the understatement of the year competition!'

'Touché. Alright, we're an intolerable hoard of trash-talking tarts. Is that more accurate?'

'Much closer to the truth. And the alliteration isn't bad either—for a trash-talking tart.'

'You spoil me with your compliments, good sir,' Hadassah said with a mock bow.

Hegai was pleased to find a beauty with wit. 'Sir? I'm not used to being called a "sir".'

'Do you mind?'

'No. It's nice.'

'Then, I shall continue,' she said with a smile. 'I'll also find words that alliterate with it.'

'Allow me to alleviate all your alliterating aspirations,' Hegai responded, forcing a giggle from Hadassah.

'How so?'

Hegai thought for a second. 'I think "the singularly sagacious sir" would be an acceptable form of address.'

'I think, sir, you're asking a bit much.'

'Okay. 'Sir' is far better than the other names I'm called around here!'

Thus began an unusual friendship. During the Achaemenid dynasty, these associations were rare. A trusted eunuch wielded

The Girl and the Guardian

lots of authority. Hierarchies of prominence also formed within a harem and more than one concubine had conspired seditiously with a eunuch. The relationship between eunuch and concubine was usually cold at best and often seasoned with scorn.

Esther's newfound humility created emotional space for genuine empathy—and this made an impact on Hegai. He repaid her kindness with upgraded sleeping quarters, diet tips, and servants. But, the most valuable thing of all was that he gave her insights about how to seduce the planet's most powerful playboy.

28

THE WEEKS AND months flowed onward. Esther flourished in the harem as Heaven worked to soften her heart and bless her through her friendship with Hegai. Meanwhile, Mordecai had good days when he trusted Heaven's goodness—and bad days when all was dark. Through all this, Jeremiah proved himself a faithful friend; a friend that sticks closer than a brother.

'It's all my fault, Jere. I'm the worst guardian in Jewish history.'

Jeremiah shook his head. 'No, it's not your fault. Don't kick yourself.'

'If I'd only moved us to Israel, or at least married her off sooner, they'd never have taken her. Now she's locked in a pagan harem for the rest of her life—never to enjoy a free life or build a family.'

'Okay, when you put it like that, it is your fault. Morty the Monster. We'll stone you at dawn.'

Mordecai recognised his friend's humour but couldn't find the strength to chuckle. 'Yeah. I deserve that.'

The Girl and the Guardian

Jeremiah sighed. 'Stop it! You're doing that self-pity thing again. You might as well take a dump in your hand and slap yourself with it. The Mordecai I know never did self-pity. Hadassah's kidnapping was a tragedy. We feel terrible for her and you. But it's been nine months. There's nothing you can do.'

'Is that what you think I need to hear—that it's time to move on?'

'If you don't, I'll kick you forward.'

Mordecai had marched through all the emotional peaks and swamps that come with losing someone dear to you. He'd entertained the impossible hope that he might rescue her and had wept over her grim future as a sex-slave. At times, whenever he turned inward, his sense of failure would crush him.

'Let's think of something positive. You're still getting news, right?'

A slight but reluctant smile appeared. 'Yes. I still get morsels from the rumour mill by the palace.'

'Great! So, what's the latest?'

'So, like I said last time, the eunuch I know tells me that a girl named Esther made quite an impression on people early on. Apparently, she's even befriended Hegai himself, the chief eunuch who keeps the royal harem.'

'That's right, Hadassah, the feisty nationalist. I couldn't believe it when you told me. How she became besties with a pagan eunuch, I'll never know.'

'I used to tell her a righteous person could still have gentile friends. I never thought she was listening.'

'This was good news. Right?'

'Certainly,' Mordecai acknowledged, 'But in the long run, will it make any difference? She's a Jewish virgin in a pagan contest.'

'She's clever, she might think of something.'

'What? Is she gonna sit down and schmooze him with a few Jewish jokes and a good sales pitch? Not likely. As of two months ago, the contest officially began. The girls have begun their nights with the King. If it hasn't happened already, it will soon be Hadassah's turn, and then they'll relegate her to to the royal harem for the rest of her life.'

Jeremiah added. 'It looks dark. I mean, she's about to have sex with the most powerful playboy in the world, she's a teenager, the King is forty, and her whole future depends on her knocking his over-sexed socks off. She's also trying to hide her Jewish identity, which is a whole other layer of challenge that's probably stressing her out of her mind. Let's not forget that she has to eat non-kosher foods—probably every single day, and—'

'Jere...Too many details.'

'Ah, right. Sorry, Morty.'

'Don't you see? Even if she has befriended the chief eunuch, what difference would that make? The other girls grew up in environments that celebrate immorality.'

'Fair point. She wasn't exactly learning bedroom tricks at synagogue school.'

Mordecai moaned. 'It's impossible.'

'Not impossible. Hadassah's still got her, um, assets,' Jeremiah said with half a grin.

'I'm choosing to ignore that.'

'Probably for the best.'

Mordecai sighed. 'At least the palace will supply all her material needs. Her life will be a lonely one, and she'll never know the embrace of a husband or the security of family life. But she'll never starve. She'll be safe.'

'I don't know, Morty. Maybe she's in there right now, enjoying a pastry, and a good laugh with the other girls.'

'Don't, Jere. We both know that's not true.'

'Okay, I'll stop. But let's not give up. We can pray.'

'Pray? How? Pray that Heaven would help a Jewish maiden bang a pagan King into hitherto unexperienced sexual bliss? Heaven doesn't work that way.'

'Heaven has a funny way of deciding for itself how it works.'

'Yes…it does. You're right. We should pray. But still, being in that harem is probably violating her conscience in all sorts of ways.'

***

'THAT WAS AMAZING!' Xerxes roared in astonishment. Esther returned his praise with a confident wink—as if to say, *There's more where that came from.*

Radiating contentment, the King gazed at Esther's olive nakedness with its mesmerizing hills and seductive valleys. He

The Oliver Anderson Trilogy

looked at her oval face, honeyed with sweat, nostrils flaring from the exhilaration of their activity moments earlier. Her dark eyes were wide and beguiling, and her red lips pressed together in a subtle smile.

He leaned back on a pillow with his hands behind his head and smiled. 'How'd you like to be Queen?'

29

'WAIT, GRANDPA. HOW did she wow the King? What did she do exactly? I'm mean, he was used to some pretty wild stuff, right? What does the Bible say?'

'I'm glad to hear yer eager to know what the Bible says, but Scripture doesn't list the techniques she used. It gives us no titillating details, I'm afraid. All it says is that she followed Hegai's instructions.'

'Still, it's amazing that she won.'

'She had Hegai's best insights and some praying friends. But, yes, it was remarkable. We're ignorant of how she did it though.'

'Shame! If Esther and Hegai could write a book on sex tips, they'd make millions. Call it 50 Shades of Persia. Why do you think the King fell for her?'

'Why does any man fall for any woman? A look? A smell? A unique personality flair? An arrow from Cupid's bow? The romantic in me wants to think Esther brought in a musical instrument to play for him or somethin' that set her apart from the predictable sex toys the other girls would've brought.

Perhaps they conversed. Xerxes probably wanted to know that his future queen at least had a nice demeanour, intelligence, and charm. Even if Esther was a wild cat in the bedroom, the King still didn't want a Vashti 2.0.'

'So it was more than sex?'

'I like to thinks so.'

'But we don't know?'

'Perhaps it was somethin' in her conversation. But don't kid yerself. If it's a turd, don't polish it. Esther spent the last year covered in lotions and myrrh—not studyin' philosophy. Xerxes' choice probably involved more than merely good sex. But ye can bet it was some blow-your-eyeballs-out lovemakin'.'

'These old stories aren't as dull as I'd thought,' Oliver said, leaning back in his chair. 'But this ending is a bit too Disney. You know, a common girl becomes a princess. It's been done before. The story was thoughtful, but I'm still not sure where to go with this script.'

'Who says the story's over?'

'There's more?'

'We're not even close to the end, laddie.'

'Something happens after she becomes the Queen?'

'Yes, but before we go there, what do ye have against a happy endin' in a story. If I had said, "And they all lived happily ever after", wouldn't that have been lovely?'

'It's all a bit predictable. Plus, life isn't like that.'

'Is it not?' William asked without a hint of sarcasm.

'No! Not at all! This is the real world where people suffer, die, and their lives don't always have happy endings.'

William wrapped his hands around his mug and looked down into its darkness. 'The Bible acknowledges all that pain and perplexity. It's filled with stories of sufferin'. But the Bible is about life in this world and, in this world, there's always more story. The unhappy endin' of one chapter flows into a new one of unknown quality. Hadassah, the Jewish schoolgirl, is kidnapped, but she is becomin' Esther, Queen of the Persian Empire. The Bible deals with human darkness, but it's not pessimistic. Aye, ye will probably never experience changes in this life as dramatic as Esther did. But the gospel promises are mind-blowin' despite all the sufferin'. They describe love and treasures beyond what we can imagine.'

'But life is hard, I'm only earning slightly more than minimum wage, and I haven't had a girlfriend in over a year. It's hard to see any good even at a far distance. I'm simply not feeling love and treasure.'

The crow's-feet crags at the corners of William's eye gathered as he looked intently at his grandson. 'Christians live by hope!' he declared in a preaching voice.

'Hope? I'd prefer something that makes a difference.'

'Hope makes the biggest difference of all.'

'How?'

'Suppose I hire two men to work for me. I tell the first that if he works all day, I'll buy him a pint. He comes to work, and the conditions are terrible. It's hot, sweaty, and coworkers are mockin' him. The work is much harder than he imagined. What happens? Ye can probably guess. After the first hour, he quits.'

'No pint is worth that.'

'Aye, exactly. But I tell the second guy that if he works for me all day, I'll give him the most excellent pub in all of London. He comes to work, and it's the same poor conditions. But he doesn't mind. Co-workers are still mockin' him, it's hot and sweaty—but he's happy the whole day long. The first guy complained. The second whistled. What's the difference?'

'Hope?'

'Aye. The two men have different attitudes based on their understanding of their final destination.'

'I get it. You're saying that what someone believes about the future effects how they handle difficulties in the present.'

'Not bad for a Londoner.'

Oliver gave another silent laugh. 'Glad to hear it. If I believed what you believe about the future, I'd live differently too—or, at least, I'd feel different about life.'

'Maybe one day ye will be. Now, stop with yer interruptions. Our story's not endin'. It's just gettin' started.'

'I am curious, but I should get back to writing my project.'

'Do you want me to stop?' William asked.

Oliver thought before responding. 'The whole reason I came up here was to finish my script.'

'Okay. I'll let ye be.'

The Girl and the Guardian

'But,' Oliver hesitated, 'I still don't know what to write. And, well, I am curious to know how Hadassah gets on as the Queen. So… let's continue. At least, for a bit.'

'Alrighty then,' William roared. 'Back to Persia, it is!'

30

TRUMPETS ECHOED THROUGH the city and the Empire as messengers carried the news: 'The Emperor had chosen a Queen, Esther by name! Feasting shall take place in her honour, and the Emperor will suspend taxes!' For fifty million people, this was good news. It was, at the very least, a chance to get off work and party. But, for one man in the Jewish quarter, the news came crashing down upon him like an avalanche.

'Morty! Did you hear?' Miriam said panting, as she exploded through his door with Jeremiah coming a few seconds later, panting even heavier. Mordecai turned his head and stared right at them.

'Morty, the news … could it be?'

Slowly Mordecai opened his mouth. 'You're here. Poke me, slap me, kick me—something. I need to know that I'm awake.'

'You're awake Morty,' Miriam said, coming over and putting a hand on his shoulder. 'We ran here the moment we heard the messengers.'

The Girl and the Guardian

'Morty, what are the chances?' Jeremiah asked. 'You've been getting news from the harem. Are there any other Esthers in the contest?'

Mordecai shook his head before any noise managed to come out. 'It's a common enough name, but no. The eunuchs have told me there's just one. It must be her. But ... how?'

'Well, we prayed, didn't we?'

'Yeah, but I didn't think—'

'Write this down, Miriam. I was right, and Morty was wrong about something. This doesn't happen often—as in ever.'

Mordecai's look of bewilderment didn't fade. 'But how?'

'Told you she's got some excellent assets—Ouch!' Jeremiah winced as Miriam pulled her arm back for a second slap. 'I mean she's got a great personality! Her sense of humour probably impressed the King. Really, what do you think I meant, babes?'

Miriam lowered her hand and folded her arms across her chest. She tilted her head forward, giving him the infamous female cold stare

Jeremiah turned his attention to Mordecai. 'What do we do now? Can we see her again? Can you visit her in the palace? Heck, could she come down here? Think babes, we could have royalty over for dinner.'

Mordecai stared out the window. Jeremiah knew when his friend's wheels were spinning. Finally, he opened his mouth, 'No. We can't.'

Miriam lowered her arms. 'But why? If she's the Queen, she could—'

'No, she couldn't. Or more precisely, she shouldn't.'

'But why?'

'Growing up, I instructed her to keep her Jewish identity secret outside of the neighbourhood. You know what it's like out there.'

Jeremiah protested, 'But now that we have a Jewess on the throne, we're in a safer position than ever. We've got royal protection!'

Mordecai slowly nodded his head. 'Yes. It would seem that way. But not in the long term. Think, Jeremiah, how long do these Empires last? First, it was Babylon. Then Cyrus and his son established Persian rule. But what happened to Cyrus' son? We still don't know. Suddenly Darius, the lance bearer, is the new King—and now Xerxes. How long before this dynasty or this Empire gets overthrown? If it's known that Xerxes' new bride is Jewish, all of his enemies become our enemies. A warring Empire or an enemy faction within Persia would see all Jews as being loyal to Xerxes—they'd eliminate us if they ever eliminated him.'

Miriam's brow furrowed. 'So this means we can't visit? That you—'

'It's not best for our people. Hadassah will guess that. Heaven knows I've explained Persian politics to her over countless meals.'

The Girl and the Guardian

Miriam drew close to Mordecai and wrapped her arms around him. 'I'm so sorry. I got all excited for her and then for you. But, what you're saying, is that ...' a tear came down her cheek as she struggled to finish.

Mordecai placed his hand on top of Miriam's, and looked up into her eyes. 'I want to see her more than anything. But I'd be risking our people to serve my own desires if I did. No, she's safe now—I have to move on.'

Jeremiah gave his friend a nod of admiration. 'He's right, babes. It's a sacrifice, but this whole world of Persian power is some crazy and dangerous stuff—and Morty knows it better than most.'

Mordecai chuckled.

'What's funny?' Miriam asked, astonished to hear him laugh.

'She won!'

'Yes!' Jeremiah exclaimed.

'Even if we don't see her, this is still a miracle. Heaven's up to something—I just don't know what. In the meantime, the King has called for feasting and drinking in the new Queen's honour, so that's what we'll do!'

Jeremiah nodded. 'That's my Morty!'

The Oliver Anderson Trilogy

31

IT WASN'T ANY old feast. Not with the great King. Xerxes gonna Xerxes. He is so smitten with Esther that he sets about to throw the most fabulous wedding reception in history—inviting all the aristocrats and everyone who worked for the Persian government. He even cancelled taxes.

The feast was outside in the gardens near the palace. Everything was in bloom. It touched Esther as both a sweet gesture by her new husband and also as an excellent opportunity to make friends with women in the aristocratic world that would be her new home. But, on the day, the reality was a bit overwhelming. Esther wasn't incredibly introverted, but there was a continual queue of girls and women wanting to introduce themselves to the new monarch. Though she loved the garden setting, the socialising was stiff and formal beyond anything she'd endured before. She spoke with dozens of ladies without feeling like she'd met a single human being. Barely an hour into it and Esther wanted to retreat to her quarters.

'How dreadful to be the new Queen!'

The Girl and the Guardian

Esther's eyes jumped up to the pretty girl standing in front of her.

'Excuse me, what did you say?'

'Being the new Queen must be abysmal!'

Esther fought for the appropriate words with which to respond, but they fluttered out of her reach.

'Tiger got your tongue?' the girl asked with a wink.

'Wh-why would you say that?'

'You know, I can't imagine having to clean that whole palace! The dusting alone must take a week.'

And, with that, Esther broke out into the first laugh she'd had all day. Tension floated off her shoulders, 'Thank you for queuing up to volunteer your services, stranger. I'll see you at 6 am sharp, and we'll start dusting the north wing.'

The stranger smiled. 'Hi, my name's Sabina,' she said in a voice quickly shedding its posh aristocratic airs.

'Hi, I'm Esther.'

'Yeah. I know. Everyone knows.'

'Of course,' she replied with embarrassment, as she sought to adapt to the breath of fresh air standing in front of her.

'It was a joke—about the Queenship being dreadful.'

'Yes, I figured. Thanks'

'For what?'

Esther sighed. 'I needed a laugh.'

'You're quite welcome. Is this party wearing you out?'

'Yes, it is. Far too many to meet all at once.'

'I thought so. Bet you're ready to escape back to the palace.'

The Oliver Anderson Trilogy

'Exactly! How could you tell?'

'The look in your eyes.'

Esther bit her lip. The idea that a stranger could see what she was feeling both thrilled and terrified her. Only Mordecai had a knack for reading her thoughts, and they'd lived together for almost six years. Though she ached for someone to genuinely know her, she had no desire to have strangers peeking inside.

Sabina broke the awkward pause. 'At least the pastries are good. The palace makes the best.'

'So true! I've been in there over a year, and I'm still not tired of them.'

'I know today is full on. When you've settled in, we can meet up and talk. You much of a horse rider?'

'I sure am,' Hadassah exaggerated. She'd only ridden twice in her life. 'When's good for you?'

Sabina smiled. It was clear the new Queen, from a non-aristocrat background, wasn't used to having servants arrange her social calendar. 'I'll have my people contact your people, and we'll set up a date,' she replied with a kind smile.

Esther nodded, remembering her servants. 'Thank you.'

'You know something, Queeny?'

Esther smiled with curiosity. 'What?'

'You're not nearly as ugly as everyone says.'

Esther's jaw dropped.

Sabina laughed. 'I jest! You're absolutely enchanting, and you know it. Relax. This party won't last forever.'

Esther smiled. 'Yes, you're right. Thanks again.'

The Girl and the Guardian

'I better go. There's a long line of boring, middle-aged women behind me who are pretending to want to meet you—they're actually jealous and secretly hate you.'

Esther rolled her eyes. 'Swell.'

'Better you than me. See ya, Queeny.'

And off Sabina went leaving Esther with fresh hope that she might find a friend in this bizarre new world after all.

32

THE WEEKS AND months flew by in her new role. Esther was grateful for the servants who guided her in all the court etiquette and expectations people had of a Persian Queen. She soon discovered that the Persian court could be both complicated and dangerous—with political posturing for Xerxes' favour being the full-time practice of the elite. Arrogant aristocrats, power-driven satraps, the mystical magi, and seductive courtesans all had their revolving role in the dance around the one who sat at the centre of the Persian universe: Xerxes.

And it was he that Esther was trying to find as she turned a corner and headed towards the centre of the palace where the throne room and adjoining rooms dedicated to the affairs of State were located. Behind her marched two eunuch warriors with swords who accompanied her about the palace every time she left the Queen's quarters.

Esther hadn't seen her husband for two weeks—the most extended time yet since their wedding. Usually, he would come to check on her welfare, to see how she was doing, to join her

The Girl and the Guardian

for a meal, or to make love. But, as fourteen days had gone by without a word, she felt frustrated and went hunting for her husband.

She put on her court attire and worked her way through the palace to where the officials did their government business. As she approached where she expected he might be, Esther recognised a eunuch who was walking in the opposite direction, carrying messages inscribed on clay tablets.

'Your Majesty,' the eunuch said as he bowed upon approaching her. He rose, intending to continue.

'Wait a moment, please,' Esther requested.

The eunuch stopped and turned to face her, bowing again. 'Yes, Your Majesty. How might I be of service to you?'

Four months into her role and Esther still felt shy in the face of such deference. 'Your name is Hathach, am I right?'

'Yes, Your Majesty. You honour me by remembering it—as you have so many names to learn in this new world.'

Esther appreciated his kind words. 'Are you busy at this moment?'

'I am taking a message from the magi order to the royal counsellors.'

Though she was eager to ask about her husband, Hathach's errand sparked a curiosity within her. 'Are you a mage yourself?'

'Some of the magi have schooled me and allowed me insight. I am considered an apprentice in the magical arts, but I'm not a full mage—I am not able to cast any spells for you if that is what you're wondering. I'm just an eager student of the stars and the elements. My job, however, is to serve as a royal messenger.'

'What is the magi's message to my husband's counsellors?'

Hathach stood tall as if he was making a grand pronouncement. 'The stars speak of threats from a dragon.'

Esther smiled. 'A dragon? I confess to having never seen one.'

'Not all dragons have the appearance of a dragon. At times they appear as lambs. Do you listen to the stars, Your Majesty? With a name like Esther, I imagine your family must be devout. Is your father a stargazer?'

'My father taught me to look for guidance from the Maker of the stars more than the stars themselves.'

Her words intrigued Hathach. He wasn't used to dealing with royalty who said such things. 'And who do you believe this Maker is, Your Majesty?'

Esther knew she was close to saying too much and changed the subject back to the purpose she initially had stopped him for. 'Perhaps we can discuss the identity of this Maker another time, my dear messenger. Is it true that I often see you near my husband when he's sitting at court?'

'Yes. As a royal messenger, I often have the honour of serving His Imperial Majesty.'

Esther gave a relieved sigh. 'Thank you. I am looking for my husband. Do you know where I can find him?'

Hathach paused, unsure of how to respond. 'Is there an emergency, Your Majesty?'

The Girl and the Guardian

'An emergency? Well, no, I suppose not. But it's been several days since we've seen each other and I wanted to speak with him.'

Hathach bit his lip before responding. 'Your Majesty is new to court protocol. Perhaps you are unaware that no one approaches the King without being invited.'

Esther smiled in disbelief. 'Yes, I have heard this—but surely this can't apply to the Queen.'

Hathach responded with a serious face.

'Wait. Does it?'

'I am afraid so, Your Majesty.

'But that's crazy!'

'It is how things operate here.'

'But why?'

Hathach took a deep breath. 'There are many reasons. We honour the King by letting him decided who he keeps company with and when. The Immortal guards also see this as a way of protecting him. King Xerxes has many enemies, and some have attempted to assassinate him. That's why the guards only allow people into his presence that he, himself, has invited.'

'I see.'

'Your Majesty, if there is an emergency, I am authorised to carry messages both to and from him.'

Esther paused, absorbing the reality of this martial dynamic. 'Well, can you let him know that I'd like to see him again,' she muttered in a vulnerable tone.

'I shall deliver the message, but His Imperial Highness decides his schedule for himself.'

'Of course. I'm sure once Xerxes hears, he'll come to see me.'

Hathach gave no reply.

Esther felt uncomfortable and filled the silence with her internal processing. 'I imagine he must be busy running the Empire. I suppose the honeymoon and the feasting can't go on forever—can it?'

'No, Your Majesty,' Hathach said sympathetically. 'I am sure His Majesty will come and see you once he's ready.'

Esther found reassurance in Hathach's firm yet kind demeanour. 'Yes, of course he will. I guess I'm a bit impatient, that's all.'

Hathach smiled with understanding eyes.

'Might I ask, finally, what the King is up to today?'

'Your Majesty?'

'Are you aware of what business my husband's engaged with?'

Hatach became suddenly stiff. 'I am aware, Your Majesty.'

'Well? Please tell me. I'm curious about what business my husband is overseeing.'

'He's,' Hathach paused, clearly uncomfortable. 'I'm not sure it's my place to say, Your Majesty.'

Now she felt annoyed. She had accepted the eunuch's words up till now, but she refused to accept that she couldn't know what business her husband was engaged in.

The Girl and the Guardian

Esther's dark eyes ignited, and words exploded out of her mouth. 'Hathach! I'm the Queen. I insist you tell me what is keeping my husband away. Is he travelling? Is he dealing with military matters? Matters of State? Internal politics? Please at least tell me where he is. I'm the Queen, and I deserve to know.'

Hathach gave a respectful but uncomfortable nod. 'It is your right. And, as you've insisted, I must answer.'

'Well, I'm glad we understand each other then. Where's my husband?'

'Your husband is in the royal harem, Your Majesty.'

Esther opened her mouth, but it failed to formulate anything comprehensible. She felt small and stupid and wished she hadn't embarrassed herself by asking.

Hathach could see the pain in her eyes. This was not what the new Queen had been hoping to hear. 'Have I upset you, Your Majesty?'

'It's never fun when your myths dissolve,' she said after an awkward pause. She gazed down the marble floor. 'Thank you for informing me, Hathach. You may deliver your star messages to the royal counsellors.'

Hathach felt for her and wanted to say more, but he knew that it was not his place. 'Thank you, Your Majesty,' he said with a bow and proceeded down the hall.

***

Esther returned to her quarters, where she threw pillows and swear words against the walls. *Stupid Hadassah! Foolish Hadassah! What were you thinking?! That this pagan pig would*

127

never bang the tarts in his harem again? That all the mistresses would go away? What's the point of even being the wife of a man like this!

She had her servants draw a hotter than usual bath. Once inside, she added her own tears to the water. She scrubbed her body with an African pumice brush. Usually, she avoided that harsh, abrasive feel. But today she needed the hot water and volcanic stone to give her a sense of cleansing that went deeper than just her almond skin—as though it was possible to exfoliate away the stain of everything Persian.

It was then, sitting in the bath, that she remembered Sabina from the wedding feast. She, at least, had treated her like a human being and not merely a monarch people bowed at. Sabina had wanted to spend time with her. And, right now, that's all Esther desired: for someone to want her.

The Girl and the Guardian

33

'I ALWAYS THOUGHT royal life must suck.'

William sipped the black java. 'It has its perks. But, yes, it can be lonely.'

'Is she in love with Xerxes?'

'At first, Xerxes seemed to love her. The Bible records that he chose her out of all the other girls. He also threw that huge feast for her. But history records Xerxes as havin' reckless addictions—his harem bein' one of them.'

'The film 300 left me with the impression that Xerxes had all sorts of kinky fetishes. Must've been weird for Esther.'

'For a devout, Jewish lass like her, it would've been a rollercoaster of emotions. At first, she despised Xerxes as an immoral gentile. Then he, the most powerful man in the world, picks her to be his wife. That must've felt nice. But then, not too far into their marriage, he's divin' right back into his harem without payin' her any attention.'

'Why would you need a harem when you have a babe like Esther?'

'That's not how it works. Lust makes ye want what ye don't have. Sexual desire is good and healthy. But, when it twists into an all-consumin' lust, it demands continual novelty.'

'She must've thought she could tame him though—like when Beauty kisses the Beast. That's what girls want, right? They want to use their feminine wiles to tame the wild man.'

William smiled. 'A girl can dream, can't she? Esther was a clever girl. She must've known that the love was never going to be greater than the lover givin' it. An impulsive man can only give an impulsive love, and a superficial man can only give a superficial love—even if it's sincere. Xerxes loved Esther more than the other girls from the contest. But he loved her for his own honour and his own pleasure—he didn't love her for herself.'

'Damn. That's painful to learn.'

'Aye. Such a life feels damned. But Esther isn't alone. Millions have discovered loneliness deeper after marriage than before.'

'At least she found one new friend. Will she and Sabina become besties?'

'We'll see how that goes.'

34

MORDECAI SET OUT towards Jeremiah's house one evening during Persia's short, cool winter season. Ever since Hadassah's kidnapping, he and Miriam had been diligent in having Mordecai over for dinner—so that he wouldn't have to eat alone. Occasionally, they'd invite one of Miriam's single friends too in hopes of getting him married—all without success.

Since his cousin's exaltation to the throne, Mordecai had vacillated between good days, when he was happy for Esther's glorious circumstances, and lonely days when he only thought of her absence. Today was one of the latter. As he sludged along through his puddles of self-pity, he reflected on a question: *why do I serve a King who's taken the most precious person in the world from me?* It was a question that cut deep. Being a godly witness in a pagan world had been a vision that Heaven had renewed in his life since childhood. Still, if anything could kill that vision, it was the kidnapping of his cousin.

When he was only a few minutes away, another thought inserted itself: *you've left your cloak back at work.* He paused for a moment as the internal debate occurred within him. *Do I*

131

turn around to get it now or do I leave it for tomorrow? He decided to turn back.

When he got to the gates, he went to a side room where department directors could leave their outdoor wear. His cloak hung on the hook where he had left it. He reached for it.

Voices leaked through the wall. Whispers—the content of which grabbed his attention and sent his heart racing. They spoke of the King, and not in a good way. He held his breath and strained to listen.

'Where will the knife be?'

'In the place we discussed.'

'I can't wait. Two more weeks and justice will finally be ours. The King will pay for his crimes and oppression.'

'Careful, Bigtham. We can't get sloppy. We need to cover every last track if we're to appear innocent.'

The higher than normal voices made him think they were eunuchs—though that can be harder to discern when people are whispering. They soon finished the conversation and then left. He missed many of the details, but he had a name: Bigtham.

He stood still for a moment, digesting what he'd heard. As he contemplated what to do, something inside of Mordecai told him to walk away.

Why should you care what happens to this King?

This drunken pagan took Hadassah from you when he already had a harem full of women. Let him die. Perhaps in the chaos that would ensue, you'll be able to get Hadassah back. It's fair.

It's justice!

Mordecai wrestled with a temptation fiercer than any he had ever faced. It was as if the universe itself was in the balance. The inner voice continued, *The King deserves what's coming to him. It's not like you're doing it. All you need to do it stay out of the way.* Mordecai held tightly to his cloak as he turned to leave the room for Jeremiah's.

He took his first step. As soon as he did, another voice, strong and clear, rang above his thoughts. *The Lord is merciful and gracious, slow to anger, and full of mercy.* The declaration brought him to a sudden halt. His mind lifted, and he caught a glimpse of the character of Heaven.

He was suddenly awed and ashamed. The light of glory illuminated his own ambition, cowardice, and growing bitterness. He realized that Heaven was treating his corrupted heart with undeserved mercy—a mercy he wasn't showing others.

He pivoted on his foot and began to walk, not towards Jeremiah's, but back towards his office. He had a letter to write. But he wouldn't send it to the King's Immortal bodyguards as one normally would in such circumstances. He would send it elsewhere. It was a risk. But he knew, if it worked, that it would be worth it.

***

'I love what you've done with the place since you first moved in. It was so drab when you took over.' Sabina said as she took another morsel of pastry from a servant who stood nearby.

'Well, the previous Queen hadn't lived in them for over four years.'

'Yes, but they looked dull even when she was here.'

'You were in these quarters when Vashti was Queen? How?'

'I was only eight at the time, but I remember how it looked. My older sister was friends, if 'friends' is the right word, with Her Highness. I came here with her once—shortly before the King banished her.'

'Your older sister knew Vashti?'

'Yes. They're alike.'

'How so?'

'Let's say that some women are white wine in a glass while others are piss in a clay cup.'

'I'm sure neither are that bad!'

'Truly. Vashti and my sister are both painfully obnoxious. Plus, they're both old.'

'How old?'

'My sister's thirty-two. Vashti's about the same.'

'Kind of old for a sister, I guess.'

'I, for one, am glad Xerxes nabbed a younger wife. Now, I get to chill with the Queen! Trust me, babe: both the change in décor and the change in Queens was for the best.'

'What was she like? Vashti, I mean.'

The Girl and the Guardian

'Besides being old and nasty? How about uptight and power-hungry?'

'Nevermind. I shouldn't have asked that question. I shouldn't gossip about a former Queen of Persia.'

'A former Queen and your husband's ex. Oh, I could tell you a juicy story or two about her. For example, did you know—'

Esther squealed with laughter. 'Stop it, Sabina! I can't. I don't want to know these stories—even if she was the most horrid woman ever to wear the crown.'

'Anything you say, Queeny.'

To say Esther enjoyed her new friendship with Sabina would be putting it mildly. It had captivated her. Even in synagogue school, Esther never had female company this electric. Sabina seemed to read her as well as Mordecai ever could, and yet it had a wild quality about it that made it unique.

'What was your family like?' Sabina asked. 'I still know nothing about your background.'

'There's not much to tell compared to the glamour of the aristocrat world. I'm sure you'd find it dull.'

'I'm so bored of being around aristocrats. That's what I like about you—you're different. Come on, tell me. Let's start with your dad. What does he do?'

Esther had become adept at talking her way out of answering such questions about her history. But Sabina was pressuring her more than anyone else had yet. The issue split her in half. Part of her wanted to ride the emotive wave and be fully transparent with her new soul mate. The other part knew she needed to follow Mordecai's instruction and keep her identity private. Esther's mind raced for something to say, but she drew blank. *Heaven, help me.*

Just then, a maidservant entered the room and bowed. 'Excuse me, Your Majesty. A girl from the bakery gave me this letter. She said a eunuch had given it to her. I apologise if the letter is in any way inappropriate, but she told me it was urgent.' She handed the letter to the Queen.

Sabina laughed. 'An urgent letter? What on earth?'

Esther's eyes grew wide, and her palms sweaty. It was like an axe that chopped open a frozen river inside of her. And that was before she even opened it.

'What's that? Is it a letter from someone you know?'

Esther made a snap decision. She needed to be alone. 'I'm so sorry dear. Important palace business has fallen on my lap, and I must attend to it. Let's reschedule for your place soon.'

Sabina put on her best teenage girl pout face. 'Must we?'

'I'm afraid we must. It's urgent.'

'Okay, darling. You're the Queen.' With that, Sabina got up off her sofa and sauntered across the room, followed by her maidservant. 'Chao for now, my love.' She blew Esther a kiss and left.

'Chao.'

Esther stared at the letter. She had grown accustomed to having no communication from the man who was dearest to her in the world. But now she trembled at the sight of his seal. So much has happened over the last two years!

She breathed out. 'Mordecai.' *Why's he writing? Isn't this a risk?* That other life she had said good-bye to and emotionally buried now called out to her from beyond that inner grave.

The servants were still standing at attention. 'Leave me!' she commanded. As soon as they had left, she tore the letter open. After a brief congratulations at marriage and queenship, Mordecai launched into his description of an assassination attempt. *My husband!* She trembled and continued to read. After her initial shock over the murder plot, she wondered, *Why is he telling me instead of the Immortals?* But, as she read to the end, it became apparent. *He's trying to help me.*

Mordecai understood court politics. Even a royal Queen wasn't immune to people's jockeying for power. By exposing this plot, Esther would win respect and influence as a newcomer within the court's tricky network of relationships.

The letter was short on personal information. *What have you been up to Morty? How's work? Found yourself a girl yet?* But, given the nature of the information sent, Esther knew such social talk was inappropriate. After two years of silence, receiving something from him assured her of his continued love. *If only this could be normal,* she sighed, knowing this letter was a life or death exception to a needed rule.

Esther knew it was no time to reminisce. She laid her nostalgia aside, called two trusted servants, and laid a plan for how to get this information to the King and the captain of the Immortals.

137

35

THE MEN WOULD have chopped up their grandmothers and sold off the pieces to increase their chances of getting so much as a smile from Xerxes. These slaves-to-ambition surrounded the Emperor who sat on his throne with his Immortal bodyguards strategically placed to intervene in a flash should anyone displease the god-king.

Not that Xerxes always attended such sessions anymore. Certain matters, however, would bring him back to the throne—his safety being among them. That's why, today at least, he was present and acting in charge.

'Have you adequately dealt with the threat?' a counsellor asked.

'We impaled Bigthan and Teresh last night, and the birds are nibbling them away as breakfast. That should limit their ability to conspire,' an Immortal replied.

'Are we certain they involved no one else?'

'We tortured them separately, and the stories matched up. They planned their assassination attempt well, but it was only the two of them.'

'Do we know why they did it?'

'One might think that they weren't grateful for the honour of being eunuchs,' Memucan quipped.

'How was the plot uncovered?' someone asked.

'Remarkably, the intelligence came from the Queen's quarters.'

'The young Queen? Discovering treachery at this level is not easy—especially for one so young,' replied another.

The King spoke for the first time. 'Does it shock you that my Queen should be clever?'

'No, Your Majesty!' many said in unison.

'Well, she surprised me!' he said with a laugh. 'It is most peculiar but also most delightful. Hathach!'

'Yes, Your Majesty,' the royal messenger said with a bow. 'I am here.'

'Did the Magi speak of a danger a few months back?'

'I reported that the Magi saw a threat from a hidden dragon being declared in the stars, Your Majesty.'

'Do you think this is it?'

'I do not know, I would have to ask the Magi leaders themselves. Dragons can take many forms—assassins are only one of them.'

Haman stepped out of the sidelines and into the middle of the room. 'The stars are often vague in what they say, Your Majesty,' he said, giving Hathach with a dismissive glance. 'We should give praise to your Immortals for acting so quickly and to Her Majesty, the Queen, for helping to uncover the plot.'

'Does my new Queen impress you, Haman?'

'I'm sure none of us will underestimate her again,' Haman replied.

'Good. My Queen is as resourceful as she is beautiful,' the King said, turning his attention to the whole room. 'I don't, however, wish to entrust all my future safety to her alone! How can we improve our security—and by "our" security, I mean "my" security?'

Haman lived for these moments, and he was not about to let royal attention slide to anyone else so quickly. 'Your Majesty,' he said, stroking his midnight beard and bowing again. 'Ever since the Spartans set our forces back, some have dared to question the might of Your Majesty's throne—making the soil fertile for revolution. Might I suggest that Your Majesty let loose your iron sceptre here at home? Let's increase internal discipline, starting here at the capital.'

Memucan breathed an expletive into the air. The Amalekite's knack for self-promotion was no secret, and he wasn't alone in suspecting where this proposal might lead.

'Are you of the opinion that I have been too lenient with my subjects?'

'Never, Your Majesty. You rule with perfect fairness. Sadly, by stealing our victory, King Leonidas and his Greek rats have emboldened wicked hearts here at home.'

Mention of the Greeks annoyed Xerxes, but he knew his minister of information was right. 'Let's assume you're on to something, Haman. How should we increase security and

The Girl and the Guardian

discipline? It is not easy to reverse laxity in the populace—nor is finding and crushing internal dissent. Complaints would increase.'

'A lion does not concern himself with the opinions of the sheep, Your Majesty.' A line Haman had rehearsed like a theatrical flunky in case ever such an occasion arose. 'I propose that Your Majesty appoint someone he trusts to rule the capital, Susiana, and all the Empire with your glorious authority to make your righteous administrative might felt among the people.'

Xerxes looked skeptical. 'Replace the Satraps?'

'No, Your Majesty. What I propose is that you set an individual above them, one who rules with your own authority, to ensure that all the Satraps, especially the more lenient ones, enforce the old traditions and uproot sedition with an iron rod.'

'Your Majesty, if I may—' Memucan protested.

'Silence, Memucan! I want to hear what Haman has to say.' Xerxes was impetuous in his personal life, but he was no fool in political dynamics. He was well aware of Haman's ambition and was not ignorant that his slave was seeking out more power. But he also found Haman likeable. Feigning ignorance, he asked 'If I created such a role, who do you think is capable of filling it?'

The counsellors were now watching the exchange with a feeling of helplessness. Haman knew that if he was ever going to seduce the King into granting him the power he longed for, this was the time. 'Your Majesty is no mere mortal like us. You are as the gods. You alone wield the divine discernment capable of finding a man with the energy and strength to put down all rebellion and serve the glory of your majestic rule.'

Part of Xerxes felt uneasy about giving Haman the power he craved. But he found Haman to be persuasive. He did not doubt Haman's efficiency in any case. 'Okay Haman,' the King declared, 'I appoint you as chief minister over all my other servants. Viceroy and lord-mayor over Susa will be your titles.' Looking to his other advisors, he said, 'From now on, you will all respect Haman's authority as if it were my own. And, Haman—'

'Yes, Your Majesty?' Haman replied with eyes wide open, feeling the titillating effect of near-limitless human power.

'Don't displease me.'

'Yes, Your Majesty. I will ensure justice reigns.'

'I know.'

The ministers trembled. Haman's grab for power had been as sudden as it was successful. One by one they fell on their knees before the Amalekite immigrant and proclaimed, 'Hail Haman!'

The Girl and the Guardian

King Xerxes promoted Haman the Agagite,
the son of Hammedatha, and advanced him and set his throne
above all the officials who were with him.
And all the king's servants who were at the king's gate bowed
down and paid homage to Haman, for the king had so
commanded concerning him.
-Esther 3.1

The Oliver Anderson Trilogy

36

WILLIAM SLAPPED HIS hand on the table. 'Lunch?'

Oliver's body jumped and his eyes popped open. 'Ah! I mean, yes. Please. Sorry grandpa, you took me to another world there.'

'Come cook with me.'

'Sure, how can I help?'

'Put the ir'n on the flame and chuck a knob of lard in it.'

'Iron? Flame? Lard?'

'Do I need to translate everythin' into London-Speak? Put the ir'n skillet on the stovetop, light the stove with the matches, and then put a tablespoon of lard inside the skillet. I'll get the food from the fridge.'

'So lard is still a thing?'

'Ye prefer fryin' in butter?'

'Lard's fine. Sure, why not. When in Scotland, eat like an ancient warrior Celt. Kinda cool though. I can't remember the last time I cooked over a flame.'

'Well yer getin' rugged now, ain't ye?'

The Girl and the Guardian

Oliver ignored the sarcasm. 'Mum and dad have an induction cooker, but I've a microwave at my apartment.'

William's head rose and descended with noiseless laughter. 'Really? How d'ya cook steak in a microwave?'

'I don't, I suppose. What are we having for lunch?'

'I've stocked up for the weekend.' William turned from the fridge with an arm full of items wrapped in brown, butcher paper. 'We've got sausages, liver, steak, bacon, and black pudin'.'

'Um, wow, that's quite a collection of meats. Any veg?'

'Of course, we do,' the old man said, reaching into the pantry.

'Good!' Oliver said with relief.

'Here you go.'

'A can of baked beans?'

'Aye.'

'Wow, all my vegan friends in London would pass out if they could see this.'

'Pass out? Who are these vegans? Sick friends of yers?'

'No, they … nevermind. I think I still know how to light one of these things.' Oliver successfully lit the gas on his second attempt, cut off a knob of lard from the nearby block, and watched it melt on the heating skillet.

'I can't really figure Xerxes out.'

William looked over at his grandson. 'How's that?'

Well, appointing Haman as Viceroy like that—it's like putting the fox in charge of the henhouse. Isn't it?'

'Yer right. A wiser king would've dismissed Haman's snake oil. But Xerxes wasn't so prudent—he had an appetite for flattery. Haman could keep reachin' for that next rung in the glory ladder as long as he stroked the King's ego and showed efficiency. Ambition is a tricky thing. By itself, it's not evil. But the human tendency towards selfishness makes us seek after influence for our own sake and not use it for the good of others.'

'As if Xerxes wasn't crappy enough a ruler. Now this guy!'

'Xerxes may have executed his thousands, but Haman would execute many tens of thousands. The King may have known that. He handed his authority over to a serpent because he never recovered from his failure with Greece—and he'd become lazy. Haman knew that chaos creates a vacuum and that people fill vacuums with more security.'

'This can't be good news for Esther. At least she carries weight now—receiving credit for exposing the assassination. I imagine those advisors didn't want to deal with a powerful new queen.'

William began to place the meats on the heated iron. 'It wasn't what they'd encountered in Vashti, that's certain. But, yes, even with her influence in the palace, havin' an anti-Semite in power is bad news, even for Esther. The darkness has found another seat of power—and it won't be good for any Jew anywhere in the Empire.'

'Does Esther know her husband appointed Haman?'

The Girl and the Guardian

'As Queen, she would have had little to do with the practical politics of the Empire. Most likely, she was unaware that he was an Amalekite or the significance of Haman having this new position.'

'So, what does a Queen do all day? Attend ceremonies and cut ribbons?'

'Some of that, yes. But Esther also had her social network to figure out. Persian high-society was often no safer than a well-decorated crocodile pit.'

'Did Esther run into any problems?'

'Finish the cookin', and I'll tell ye about one of them.'

37

THE TWO YOUNG women led their horses to the stables. 'Servants, prepare us something to eat. We'll be ready in an hour.' Though Sabina was six months younger than her, Esther continued to find her confidence attractive. She knew what she wanted and how to get it. In the two years since they'd met, Sabina had taught the new Queen about aristocratic social life. Her care was almost maternal—filling a void for a girl raised by a single, adopted father.

Esther also valued that Sabina was, in terms of physical beauty, fully her equal. At synagogue school, Esther's beauty had sometimes made relationships with other girls a challenge. If boys were present, she'd inevitably get all their attention—much to the annoyance of other girls.

'While we wait for the food, let's go hammam.'

Esther shrugged her shoulders. 'Okay.'

***

The fragrance of flowers floated throughout the steamy atmosphere of the hammam. Sounds of water dripping and maidservants massaging their bare backs filled the room. Esther

148

closed her eyes and tried to absorb the pleasure of the moment. Between navigating the political drama of court life as well as not seeing her husband for weeks on end, Esther appreciated every happy moment that came her way.

She turned to Sabina and filled the silence. 'How's your father's search for a new fiancé coming along?'

'They struck a deal this week.'

'Your father found you a fiancé, and you haven't mentioned it yet?'

'It's only marriage. You know how dull that can be.'

Esther knew that her own marriage was less than ideal, but she refused to accept that an engagement was not something for a girl to get excited about. 'Well, I'm glad your father's finally found someone.'

'Some men are terribly reluctant to marry their daughters off.'

'Yeah, tell me about it,' Hadassah thoughtlessly said, as the memory of Mordecai's own slowness flashed through her mind.

'How would you know, Queeny?'

'Nevermind. I simply meant that the contest took a long time. But you know all about how my marriage happened. Tell me about this.'

'As I told you, Daddy broke off my last engagement months ago when he discovered he could make a deal with a more powerful family. The father has several sons, and picking the most prestigious one possible made the negotiations go on forever.'

'It's that political, huh?'

'Painfully so.'

'Well, who is it? Which family?'

'I'm to marry Aridai, one of Haman's sons.'

'Our Viceroy?'

'Of course. I'm marrying the son of your husband's best friend.'

Esther sighed. 'Haman certainly sees more of my husband than I do.'

'Trouble in paradise, Queeny?'

Esther didn't enjoy talking about her marital woes but, as she had grown close to Sabina, she found it hard not to let some of her angst out on occasion. 'Tell me all about Aridai,' she said, changing the subject.

'Daddy made a good deal. Aridai works close with his father, so marrying him ensures that I don't have to leave the city.'

'What's he like?' Esther said, glowing with a girlish grin.

'He looks handsome enough. Confident. Ambitious, like his dad. I don't know him that well. Daddy says there'll be plenty of time for that later.'

'But you are looking forward to it, right?'

'It'll be nice to command my own estate. Mother doesn't have terrible taste, but there's so much I'd do if I were the lady of the house.'

'Commanding your own interior decorating is a great perk. Anything else you're looking forward to?'

'I don't know. Men are so hard to predict.'

The Girl and the Guardian

'Indeed!'

'Romance in marriage is rare for us. Our weddings are political events. Perhaps love comes later. Grand if it does—but it's not a given.'

'I'm sorry. Reality bites sometimes.'

Sabina sat up and looked back at the servants. 'Leave us.' Esther followed her lead and sat up as well. As soon as the servants had left, Sabina faced Esther. 'We have each other though, don't we, Queeny?'

'Of course. Marrying Aridai won't change a thing.'

'But, even if our marriages do lack heat, at least we can share love.'

With that, Sabina reached over to Esther and placed her hand on Esther's well-crafted leg, leaned forward, and kissed her. Not on Esther's cheek, as customary, but long and lingering on her lips.

Esther was not naïve. Nor could she claim that this fully surprised he. Not really. She had known where this emotional wave was going—even if she had tried to ignore such thoughts consciously. What Esther wasn't entirely sure about was how she felt about it now that they had arrived at this point. She knew what was happening—and it didn't feel unpleasant. No one had kissed her with passion and desire for a long time. She felt her friend's soft body press against hers as the hand on her thigh began to move in a seductive caress.

Esther had now been three years in the heart of Persian culture. She was no longer an innocent Jewish schoolgirl. But

151

her mind still buzzed with uncertainty. Yes, this relationship was emotionally satisfying—certainly more than anything she'd had with Xerxes since the wedding. She also found there was something electric about Sabina's touch. Why shouldn't she enjoy the moment? *It's not like my husband is faithfully loving me or fulfilling my desires.*

But she knew that this wasn't who Heaven had called her to be. It took strength of elephantine proportions, but she finally managed to open her mouth. 'Sabina, wait. Let's not do this.'

Sabina backed away a few of inches with a puzzled look. 'Huh?'

Esther paused. She was unaware of how to explain this. Even if she were to reveal her identity as a Jew, it wouldn't be easy. 'It's not the type of relationship we should have.'

'Why? Don't you feel an energy between us?'

'Of course, I do.'

'Then what's the problem?'

'It's not what I'm here for,' Esther said with a hint of firmness.

A quiver rippled through Sabina's face and then quickly returned to its usual warmth and feminine confidence. 'Flings like this may not be normal where you come from, wherever that is, but it's normal among women here. Surely, being married to Xerxes, this isn't new to you.'

Esther felt the weight of her argument. Yes, these relationships were normal in palace life and especially in her husband's harem. Those concubines were never going to have husbands of their own. She learned through Hegai that her husband found such relationships a turn on. If he seeks constant refuge in his harbour of dubious delights, why can't I share love with this one woman who understands and cares for me? Here, in this hammam—with the intoxicating smell of jasmine and the light of torches flickering off the mosaic walls—she wanted to give in. She stared into Sabina's fiery eyes, famished for a deeper connection with a person she felt drawn to. In that instant, it was something she desired more than the world itself.

With a strength that didn't seem to be entirely her own, Esther moved her body a few inches away from Sabina's embrace. 'Part of me wants to say yes. I do feel drawn to you; I want to give in. But my answer must be no.'

Without appreciating the full depth from which Esther was speaking, Sabina blurted out 'Esther, don't be so reserved darling. I know that you—'

'Stop. Please.'

'Oh Queeny, what on Earth are you talking about?'

For the second time in Esther's life, she felt firm words marching out of her mouth with an authority that surprised her as she rose from the bench where they'd been sitting. 'Earth? I'm not on Earth about anything. Sabina, I've received your friendship as a gift, not merely from Earth, but from Heaven. You've been my friend, and I've always allowed you to speak to me as an equal. Perhaps this was a mistake. I did so because, being new to court life, I was hungry for a friendship that lacked the tedious formalities of court life. But please remember

The Oliver Anderson Trilogy

I'm not merely a friend. I'm also the Queen. And, though the Queenship may be lonely at times, I'll carry it with honour—not like a concubine.'

'But Queen Vashti and my sister would often—'

'I don't want to hear any stories about Vashti or what she might've done with your sister. I'm not like other girls at the palace. I'm not Vashti.' Esther said as Jewish conviction reawakened within her. Even though she was the Queen of a pagan empire, she also knew that she belonged to Heaven. 'I cannot. My body doesn't belong to me. I belong to another, and he decides.'

Sabina now stood. 'My apologies, Your Majesty. I didn't realise that my behaviour towards you was anything the King would object to.'

'Perhaps it is, perhaps it isn't. But I'm not speaking about Xerxes. As much as I feel drawn towards you right now, I know that the One who owns me, the One who created me, didn't design me for this.'

'I don't understand, Your Majesty,' Sabina said, using formality as a defence mechanism. She was usually confident standing naked in front of other women, but in the face of Esther's rebuke, she began to cover herself with her arms. She was not used to being refused, and she felt ashamed.

Esther knew she'd allowed herself to be too vulnerable to this girl in her hunger for intimate relationship. Sabina's eyes radiated anger and pain—yet Esther knew she would yield tight-lipped to her social superiority.

The Girl and the Guardian

'I must leave now, Sabina. I'm sorry my words have hurt and confused you.' With that, Esther wrapped her robe around her freshly steamed body and left the hammam. She dressed and made her way for the entrance of the house without Sabina accompanying her. She called for her servants to bring the palanquin, and they carried her off to the palace.

Esther soaked in a sea of loneliness on her ride home as tears cascaded down her freshly steamed cheeks. *Aren't I supposed to feel good when I do the right thing?* She had been getting used to palace life. But now she thought back to her synagogue friends. She longed to be in a house of worship and hear the Scriptures read. She wanted Heaven's community. She missed Mordecai.

I wonder what he's doing right now? Whatever it is, I'm sure his day hasn't been as crazy as mine.

38

'HAS ANYONE TOLD you today that you're a moron?'

'Not yet. But I've a feeling that's about to change.'

Jeremiah didn't bother to pour Mordecai a cup of wine as he reclined at one of Babak's tables. 'Well since you still don't have a wife to bust your balls, let me do it. Why do I hear that you refused to bow before the Viceroy this morning?!'

'Because it's true.'

'Well, cheers to the dumbest dummy in Dumbville.'

'Would you have bowed before that dog's anus?' Mordecai protested.

'My job isn't so high flying that I have to worry about that. Politics may not be my shtick, but even I know you're supposed to bow before the viceroy.'

'I didn't mean to not bow.'

'Are you drunk? Cause you sound drunk,' Jeremiah said in frustration. 'This isn't like you, Morty! How in the world do you "not mean to not bow", when everyone else is bowing? And before the Viceroy of freakin' Persia!'

The Girl and the Guardian

'Calm down. Okay, I did mean to. But I didn't intend to. I hadn't thought about it in advance. Haman rode by the gate on his horse, and everyone started bowing. Our national history flashed through my mind, and I felt this warmth in my chest.'

'Was it a heart attack? Because, right now, I think a heart attack might be the best thing for you.'

'It was conviction. Look, I'm the only Hebrew at the city gate. I've made compromises to be there. You understand?'

'Yes. Not full-on Jew, but Jew-ish. That's how we get by in Susa. Overthinking our national history gets Jews too radical. You know that—and you've never been that guy. You're a diplomat, not a warrior.'

'Exactly. I know how to smile and shuffle and avoid negative attention. People only know me by my Persian name. I began this career with a vision to be like Abednego and Daniel. But all I've done is be diplomatic, and a man can't spend whole his life being merely diplomatic. Conviction came. I knew this was a line I shouldn't cross. I can't bow to an Amalekite.'

'Do you imagine you're some type of Elijah-Man now? Up for some confrontation? Fancy yourself a prophet? You remember some stories from sabbath school, and suddenly you get pumped with enough chutzpah to rebuke the royals?'

'I'm not rebuking anyone. And, Elijah? Really?! I've no aspiration to be a wild desert-man in sackcloth. I'm a city-boy who keeps his beard well-trimmed, his clothes comfortable, and his relationship with the authorities respectable.'

The Oliver Anderson Trilogy

'Respectable? Well, yeah, until today. Today you stuck out like a baboon in a bath. I don't know what version of stupid you're subscribing to mate, but I admire your wholehearted commitment to it.'

'How's married life—has it caused you to forget our history? Forget what the Amalekites did to us?'

Jeremiah chugged his wine so that it ran down his beard. 'No, marriage is fine—learning to listen more. It seems wives talk. They have to process everything. Pretty sure it's hormonal. But, to your point, no! Every Jew remembers what the Amalekites did. It was unspeakable!'

'We know Haman's reputation. He's every bit like his ancestors.'

'True. Haman's a creep. In fact, to call him a creep is an offence to creeps everywhere. I wouldn't want to bow to him either, but he's a small man who casts a big shadow. I admire your bravery—.'

'I'm not brave, Jere. I'm scared,' Mordecai confessed.

Jeremiah noted his friend's vulnerable tone. 'The only time a man can be brave is when something scares him. Heck, I feel like a disgrace to my testicles compared to you right now. But not bowing to Haman, though ballsy, is a quick way to lose your job.'

'I can't disrespect our ancestors by bowing.'

'Couldn't you cough when he walks by? You know, the type that makes you lean forward a bit. Maybe you could bend to tie a sandal. A smile from him would help you gain the world.'

The Girl and the Guardian

'At the price of my soul?'

'You're gonna stand there like some gormless schmoe?'

'I respect authority. I won't speak against Haman or undermind his rule. But I can't bow. Didn't Moses declare Amalekites our enemies?'

'Long ago, Morty. Not even my mother-in-law can remember those days. His eminent creepiness has other things on his mind than our historic feud. It's Persia. We bow to kings, queens, and viceroys here.'

'Maybe the feud with the Jews is far from his mind—I hope so. But what's wrong in Israel is wrong in Susa. Even here, I can't bow to an Amalekite.'

'Didn't you used to tell Her Majesty—'

'Hadassah.'

'—Hadassah that she needs to accept Persian ways? Look at her. She's become Empress of all the freakin' pagans!'

'She had no choice. I do. We're in Persia, not of Persia.'

Jeremiah took a deep breath and reached his hand over to Mordecai's. 'I'm upset, but it's only because I worry for you.'

'And I do appreciate it.'

'As obnoxious as you are, you're the closest thing I have to a best friend.'

'Thanks. I think. I don't want this test—but I've got it. I've spent my career showing my bosses I'm a good Persian. But, if I were to kneel now, I know Heaven wouldn't be pleased.'

'Anyone ever tell you how stubborn you are?'

'Just my friends and family.'

159

39

OLIVER SHOOK HIS head as he swallowed another piece of bacon. 'It seems like neither Esther nor Mordecai are having good days at the moment.'

'Circumstances are testin' them in some painful ways—but they're comin' through the fire like gold. A truly unbearable life isn't one without pain, it's one without meanin'.'

'I'd settle for a script with some meaning.'

'If your life is full of meaning, you might find it flows out into your writin'.'

'Perhaps,' he confessed. 'You know grandpa, it was classy how Esther refused to badmouth Queen Vashti whenever Sabina brought her up. Most politicians nowadays have no problem slagging off their predecessors.'

'Yes, Vashti was as full of herself as a Russian doll. But it's usually proud people that are most offended by the pride in others. When yer truly humble, ye can be patient with anyone.'

'Why do you think the two women were so different?'

'We all have a Vashti and an Esther livin' inside of us. Yer inner Vashti wants ye to adorn yer life with diplomas, promotions, sports victories, and great relationships. She wants ye to wear yer accomplishments like merit badges that signal yer life is beautiful, and yer existence justified.'

'But accomplishments aren't bad, are they?'

'In themselves, no. Most of our goals and accomplishments are good things. But humans trap themselves whenever they make a good pursuit into an ultimate pursuit. If we're not successful, our lives descend into despair. But if we are successful, we look down on those who aren't. Yer successes are a weak foundation to build an identity on.'

'If we don't build our identity on our accomplishments, what do we build it on?'

'The Beautiful Ugly is where God changes both what and how ye love. Naturally, we love what's glorious and despise what's gruesome. We think God is the same way, so we beautify our lives with moral, religious, academic, financial, or familial achievements. Ye graduate, get married, go to church, stop looking at porn, have kids, lose fat, and build muscle. We think, Surely God will love me now!'

'Doesn't he?'

'That's how human love works. We delight in beautiful things like flowers, oceans, and lovely lasses like Esther. We despise the ugly. But God's love in Jesus is different. He doesn't love sinners because they're beautiful. He loves 'em because of what Jesus has done—because of the Beautiful Ugly—and they become beautiful by that love.'

'God loves them, and they become lovely?'

The Oliver Anderson Trilogy

'Aye. This is why our victory symbol is that cruel Roman execution stake. On its own, that ugly Tree is the most wretched of all symbols; a cruel instrument of death and decay. The miracle is that Jesus has turned this symbol into one that conveys love to millions. In beholdin' the executed Messiah, the same miracle happens in us. God pours out love on cracked and cruel hearts—and that love transforms 'em.

'That's why you call it the Beautiful Ugly?'

'Aye. It's where the beastly becomes beautiful, the deformed becomes delightful, and the loathsome becomes lovely.'

'I love the thought of it. Are you trying to persuade me to become a Christian?'

'I'd persuade the world if I could.'

'I'll be open-minded. But, first, let's finish.'

'Ye finish yer lunch. I'll take us back to Persia.'

40

'JUSTICE DEMANDS IT, Your Majesty!'

Xerxes noted the conviction in Haman's voice. 'Are you sure that we need to kill all of them?'

'Absolutely. Their backwards values and oppressive religion are cancer to the Empire—especially after all the progress we've experienced under your father's dynasty. If these people continue, your other subjects will suffer. We must act for your royal glory and the good of the many.'

Mordecai's refusal to bow had, unbeknownst to him, triggered centuries of national hatred buried deep in Haman's soul. This hatred had been on the backburner while Haman had pursued his career ambitions. But now?

Now that I am at the top, why not use this opportunity?
I can eliminate, not only this filthy piece of Hebrew rudeness at the gate but also his family and nation. It won't just be a personal justice—it will be the reaping of centuries of injustice on their part.

The Oliver Anderson Trilogy

Xerxes rubbed his chin. 'Is there another way we can bring these Jews in line?'

'Your Majesty, you appointed me as Viceroy to bring greater order to your kingdom, and these Jews are a rebellious people.' Haman knew it would not be prudent to reveal his family's historic vendetta against the Hebrew people. Such details didn't need to concern the Emperor. He knew them all—that was enough.

Xerxes was not a hundred per cent convinced by his talk of fairness and justice for the Empire. Haman did, however, have one more tool to wield. 'There is also the point of the Empire's bursary.'

'Oh?'

'For generations, Jews have exercised questionable business practices and have accumulated far more wealth than their small numbers might suggest. They don't contribute their fair share to the greater good. By eliminating them and seizing their property, I estimate that we could supply ten thousand silver talents into the royal bursary. Looting them would be an act of economic fairness.'

Xerxes' eyebrows jumped. 'Ten thousand?' That was nearly two-thirds of the Empire's income. After the war with Greece, which had been an economic nightmare, an infusion of ten thousand talents would make the Empire debt-free. 'It seems like doing justice might also be good for State finances.' The King quipped.

The Girl and the Guardian

'Nothing is better or more beautiful than justice.' Haman's plans had entrenched themselves into his conviction as an act of perfect justice. Since the Israeli King Saul had stolen the wealth of the Amalekites in his raids centuries previous, looting Jewish land and treasure were long overdue reparations.

'When do you suggest we do this?' the King asked.

Haman had rehearsed every question and objection he thought Xerxes might have. He was ready for this. 'Once I've made all the preparations, we will entrust our plans to the power of fortune by a role of the Pur-Dice—and set the date accordingly.'

'I trust fortune will be with us. You say the Jews have no army of their own?'

Haman smiled. 'They have a couple small militias based near Jerusalem, but that's it. Half of the Jewish households don't even possess a sword to guard their children or treasures with. The fools trust their money and cunning to protect them.'

'It should be easy to eliminate them,' Xerxes said thoughtfully. 'Now, are you sure about the money?'

Though Haman's ideals drove his actions, he knew that one needed to lubricate practical politics with the oil of silver to pass through even the noblest of laws. 'Yes, Your Majesty. I have reviewed the numbers myself. Shall I show them to you?'

'No Haman. That won't be necessary.' The King had long since tired of being a details guy. 'It's getting late. Go ahead with your plans. It's time to retire to the gardens for supper. Join me.'

'As you wish, Your Majesty.'

'One final thought before we do. Don't rush this. We spent two years planning to eliminate the Greeks, and it still wasn't entirely successful. If you're going to wipe out a whole ethnic group from within the Empire, make sure you've considered everything.'

'I intend to. We will not leave a single detail unexamined, Your Majesty. Only then shall I role the Pur.'

And with that, the men walked to the gardens for their wine, surrounded by servants and security. *Of course I'll take my time*, Haman mused, *vengeance is best served on a cold platter.*

The Girl and the Guardian

41

OLIVER PUSHED HIS now emptied plate across the wooden table as if it had personally offended him. 'What a dufus! Haman slandered the Jews to the King because Mordecai hurt his feelings? What is he, nine-years-old?!'

'Yes, he's one of the Bible's biggest blowhards and a cry baby. But he wasn't foolish. He told effective lies—effective because they were mixed with truth.'

'How was any of that true?'

'Contrary to Haman's fake news about them, the Jewish people weren't rebellious or revolutionary. They understood all authority comes from God. They obeyed even pagan kings— unless doing so required them to disobey God. But Haman's lie contained some truth. He described the Jews as bein' a separate people, different from the others, with their own set of laws. He understood that they were a conscious minority who didn't always conform to Persian values.'

'A "conscious minority"? You mean they were well aware of their alternative lifestyle?'

The Oliver Anderson Trilogy

'Aye. That difference was something that defined the Jews. Many of God's people still relate to Mordecai. They work, play, buy, and build relationships all within the structure of 21st Century Western society. Like the Persian Empire, the world around them has its views on God, faith, men and women, sex, food, money, violence, and the environment. With some of these things, they can agree. But, on others, they differ. They tell a different story than the world around them.'

'But it feels nice to belong to a well-defined group, doesn't it?'

'Yer right. It certainly does. But when you live within a broader culture that sees your minority views as dumb, it can be challengin'.'

'I see that.'

'Let me give you an example from somethin' I read about not long ago. Imagine some experts ask you to take a test. Not a maths or grammar test. A fun, artsy test. These experts bring ye into a room with twenty other people. Before each of ye are three pictures of three different works of art marked A, B, and C. Ye look at all three and, though they all look beautiful, yer sure that letter B is the most beautiful. Understand?'

'Got it, yeah.'

'The woman in charge asks people to say which picture they like the most and why. As they go 'round the room, you notice that no one else says B. In fact, almost everyone else says that C is clearly the best. They give reasons for why they say so: the brush strokes are more sophisticated, the colours are better

The Girl and the Guardian

coordinated, the shadin' is more elegant, etc. Now, ye feel insecure. It makes ye go back and look at the pictures. Did ye miss something? Maybe ye don't have an eye for art, and the only reason you thought B was the most beautiful was that ye weren't intelligent enough to know real art when you see it. Ye begin to get nervous as your turn approaches. Will you say B? What if by sayin' B, everyone else thinks yer ignorant about art or that ye have poor taste?'

'I'd still say B.'

'Would ye? Seventy-five per cent of the time ye would be wrong. What I read about was a test—and yer the one being tested. Everyone else in the group is in on it and have been told not to say B. Most people, even those who think they're independent or creative thinkers, go with the majority in the end.'

'So, it was hard to be a faithful Jew back then, and it's still hard to be a believer today. That it?'

'My grandson's a genius. The brains may have skipped a generation, but they're still in the family line.'

Oliver laughed. 'I'm so telling dad.'

'I bet you will.'

'I won't get you in too much trouble,' Oliver said, standing up. 'Think I need some more coffee.'

'Help yerself.'

'Has being a Christian ever cost you something?' Oliver asked over his shoulder as he turned on the electric kettle—one of the few modern conveniences in his grandfather's kitchen.

169

'Yes, but not hugely. I tend to think of what I've gained more than what I've lost. But I'd also admit that it's probably harder for young people today.'

'How so? People are free to believe whatever they want here in Britain.'

'Legally, yes, and long may it last. But social pressures have increased. Forty-five years ago, I was newly married, your dad was a baby, and I was one of the best rugby players in the area. My teammates respected me. Then, your grandmother became a Christian. I tell ye laddie, at first, I was convinced she'd been body-snatched! But she was a prayin' woman, and God changed my heart not long after. At the time, I knew that I was part of a minority—as Christians, we were a *conscious* minority. I knew most people didn't think like us. But people didn't view us as an *immoral* minority. Ye understand the difference?'

'Hmm, I don't think so.'

'For example, after a victory, when the lads on our team would go out to celebrate, it would usually involve getting drunker than I now wanted to be and often snoggin' some equally drunk lasses—and sometimes more than snoggin'.'

Oliver shrugged his shoulders. 'So? You'd party after a victory. That's normal.'

'No, it was bad. It certainly wasn't good for my marriage. As it's written, "The willy hath triumphed over sanity".'

'Is that really in the Bible?'

'I'm paraphrasing a bit. Point is, when I told my teammates that I no longer wanted to be livin' that way, I became the butt of their banter.'

Oliver returned to the table, a steaming cup now in front of him. 'So they teased you because you weren't drinking as much or cheating on grandma anymore.'

'In public, yes. Oh boy, in the locker room I'd get it. But, on the whole, the fellas didn't morally condemn me for those views. On more than one occasion I'd have a bloke come up to me, alone of course, and say somethin' along the lines of "I may not believe what ye believe, but it takes courage to be different. I respect you for that." I got teased in a group of lads, but I never felt they looked down on me as bein' bad or immoral.'

'And you think today is different?'

'I know it's different.'

'How?'

'Society no longer sees the Christian teaching on sex as morally upright. People don't privately respect you for it. If ye believe that sex is for one man and one woman in one marriage to create children and renew your covenant before God, then yer not merely wrong, yer bad. Santa's naughty list bad.'

Oliver carefully attempted his first sip of the scolding java with all the delicacy of one handling radioactive material and then placed it back on the table. 'Why do you think that is?'

'We've told ourselves a different story.'

'Story? I was never told any story about sex.'

'No? Maybe you don't know you have, but you have.'

'I'm a bit sceptical, grandpa.'

'Listen,' William said, leaning back in his chair. He looked up to the ceiling and shifted his voice into BBC narrator mode.

For hundreds of years, religious institutions squashed true love with their oppressive views of sexuality. People were not able to love who they wanted to love. Finally, the light of reason broke through. Young people rebelled against these structures. We who are now liberated have fulfilling sex lives. The teachings of bigots no longer repress us. We now love whomever and however many people we want. We self-identify however we wish, and we squash the remaining strongholds of hatred wherever we find them. Join us in our noble mission to destroy intolerance and spread sexual diversity everywhere.

William looked back down at his grandson. 'Does that story sound wholly unfamiliar?'

'No. When you put it like that, it doesn't. I couldn't tell you when I've heard that story, but I have. And thousands of times: at school, on TV, in music, online. Everywhere. I've believed that story. I still do—I think. But I'm not entirely sure why. Isn't it true?'

'Is it? Look around ye. What do ye see? Are people happier? Are children healthier? Is there less mental health issues? Are families and relationships more stable?'

The Girl and the Guardian

'Maybe not. But, if I were to become a Christian, and I'm not admitting that I'm at all interested, would that mean I need to stop having sex with girls until I marry one of them?'

'Whadda ye think Jesus would say?'

'I'm guessing he'd say that I should marry one of them before I get naked with her.'

'Is that such a terrible idea?'

'I'm not ready to get married.'

'No one said ye had to.'

Oliver's face flashed disbelief. 'I couldn't stop having sex! I mean, it's not like I get lots. But, still, I need to take what I do get.'

'I'm an old man. I've seen many people die. Not one of 'em ever died from not havin' sex.'

'Maybe it wouldn't kill me. But it would take—'

'Self-control?'

'Yes! And more than I have.'

'I appreciate yer honesty, Oliver. I'm not tryin' to give ye a hard time. Even in my day, I didn't always find it easy to follow Christ.'

'Well, it's harder today.'

'That's my whole point. If ye did make such a decision, ye wouldn't have the private respect I did. Now many people will disdain ye for your beliefs publicly and privately. It doesn't matter how polite yer about it either. I wouldn't want ye to consider followin' Jesus without knowin' the full cost. Never expect society to accept ye based on bein' a nice person. That's like expectin' a lion not to eat ye because you didn't eat it first.'

'So Haman shamed the Jews because of their differences and, if I were to follow Jesus, I might expect the same thing?'

'No need to exaggerate my point. I'm not sayin' that ye will be the object of genocide—though there are parts of the world where this happens. But don't be shocked if yer shamed.'

'Good to know. The idea of ever becoming a Christian kind of scares me now. Of course, I'm far from believing it's true—although I now see how it might be attractive.'

'That's a start. Articulatin' God's story requires a backbone made of more than chocolate eclairs. If ye embrace it, tell it—and don't apologise for it. If it's God's story, we should tell it beautifully and boldly. His story makes this world's hyped-up, technicoloured, depression-inducing story look lame by comparison.'

'Speaking of stories grandpa, I'm hoping we can—'

'Get back to Persia?'

'Like Aladdin on Red Bull.'

42

THE DAY HAD been radically, intensely, and overwhelmingly average. Mordecai's customs department had been processing new plants that had come in from various parts of the Empire—all to enhance the already exotic city gardens. As usual, the civil employees commented on the new imports.

'What's the name of this stranger?

'Says it's from the far East.'

'It says "kiwi" on the container.'

'Ugly piece of fruit. It'll never catch on here.'

And so the day passed until midafternoon. Shortly after the workers had regathered from their afternoon meal, a messenger from the Viceroy's office arrived.

'Who's that?'

'Looks to be someone from communications. Maybe one of Haman's guys.'

'Why do you say so?'

'He's carrying one of those crazy new contraptions.'

'People are calling them "scrolls", I think.'

The Oliver Anderson Trilogy

Mordecai welcomed the messenger. 'What can we do for you?'

'The Viceroy's office sent many of us throughout the city. They ordered us to break the seal on our scroll and read the message at precisely the third hour, when the trumpets blast.'

'What's it all about?'

'I don't know. It's all been tight-lipped.'

Mordecai scratched his head. 'Sounds important, but I heard nothing about it. They gave us no warning that you were coming.'

And then the trumpets blew. The messenger broke the ornate imperial seal that bound the scroll, and Mordecai called the room to attention. 'Everyone put down your plants. We've got an important message from central.'

The messenger opened the scroll, cleared his throat, and began.

His Imperial Highness, Xerxes, son of Darius does hereby call the people of the Persian Empire to a day of conquest. On the thirteenth day of the twelfth month, the month of Adar, permission is being given to kill and annihilate the Jew, the Jew's family, and the Jew's people. All Jews everywhere are to be killed: young, old, men, women, and children. Those who kill them are welcome to loot their property—so long as they place fifty per cent of all goods and coinage into the royal treasury. Failure to pay taxes on pillaged goods will result in execution.

The Girl and the Guardian

The messenger stared at the scroll for a moment after he had finished reading and then turned towards Mordecai. 'Wow. I didn't expect that. Did you?'

But Mordecai said nothing. He simply gazed at the messenger in shock. Feeling awkward as the object of Mordecai's gaze, the messenger turned away and looked out across the room. Every eye was focused on the boss.

Then, the boss whispered. 'The day of destruction has come, and I'm the one who's invited it.'

Unsure what was happening in that silent moment, the messenger left the scroll and exited the room. Slowly, something like the noise of a distant howling began to make its way into the room. The whole city had received the news. Commotion erupted. The workers spoke furiously with one another, never taking their eyes off Mordecai for too long. Those closest to Mordecai made their way to him in hopes of expressing some sort of comfort or hope, but words failed them. All they could do was stand next to their faithful executive.

Mordecai also stood, processing the message—too stunned to form whole or rational thoughts. He reached over and tore the parchment from off the scroll. Then, he turned towards the door and left the building without saying a word to anyone and headed straight back to the Jewish quarter.

Once home, he entered his bedroom, took his closes off, and opened a box where he kept sackcloth used for Yom Kippur. He had never thought to use it for any other purpose, but now he knew he needed to wear it.

177

He wandered through the Jewish quarter. Visions of his dismembered neighbours flashed before him: a mauled mother's son here, a butchered father's daughter there. He left his neighbourhood and drifted like a drugged daydream through the city, guided only by his shock.

Approaching the citadel gates, the very place he had refused to bow, he broke down. Sobs erupted from his gut. The guards would not let him enter the citadel in such a state. Not knowing what to do, he looked at them and yelled 'Is this the great running joke of our world?! A man attempts acting nobly, only to destroy what he loves? What a predictable punchline my life has become!' The guards said nothing. They seemed as immovable as the universe's intent upon cruelty.

Then Mordecai turned and collapsed like human gelatine straight into the dirt. He lifted his head and catapulted a howl from deep within his gut right through the moist March air and into the bright blue atmosphere above the citadel towers. Those nearby never forgot it. Mordecai had always said prayers for his people. Now, however, he prayed—wordless cries that kamikazed themselves right into heaven's gates. The closest he had come to weeping like this was when he lost Hadassah four years earlier. But this was more. Far more. *Doesn't Heaven care!*

***

'He ripped his clothes off and is sitting in the dirt weeping, Your Majesty,' the servant said with her head bowed. Esther had assumed it was going to be another dull day in the palace. This

The Girl and the Guardian

bit of news, however, shattered the lonely and formal humdrum that had become her daily life. Alarmed, Esther grabbed the slave's white tunic and drilled her with questions. 'How do you know this? Hold nothing back. No secrets!'

The girl's blood froze. Words flew out of her mouth so fast they betrayed her country origins. 'I'm on friendly terms with a eunuch. Nothing inappropriate, mind—hees a eunuch. Well, hees the same fella that Mordecai gave his message to, couple years back. He 'ad it, see, then he gave it to me. I was talk'n to 'im just twenty minutes back, outside the kitch'n, promise, wees only talking, and saw something wrong in hees eyes so I aks 'im and he told me he dat he'd seen 'im. All dirty and torn like.'

'Mordecai… as in my Mordecai?' Could it be another? It wasn't an unusual Persian name after all.

The servant girl took a deep breath, slowed her words down, and regained her formal palace speak. 'Yes, Your Majesty. Unless the eunuch's eyes have deceived him.'

'Well, I need you to go check.'

'Your Majesty?'

'I need you to check that it's him! Also, bring him some proper clothes!'

'Yes, Your Majesty. As you wish.'

Esther sat back down and wondered, *What's happened to you Morty?! Has there been bad news from Israel?*

***

Mordecai didn't know how many minutes or hours had passed. One cannot tell time accurately in such a state. When the servant arrived, she stood next him. He lifted his gaze to meet hers. He could tell by her dress that she was a palace slave.

She dropped a linen bag by his side. 'The Queen sent me,' she said with nervous professionalism. 'Her Majesty asks that you put these on.'

Mordecai opened the bag. *Clothes? What's Hadassah thinking? They're about to annihilate our people—and she's worried about fashion?* He looked back at the girl. 'Take the clothes back. I don't accept them.'

His words shook the servant. She wasn't used to being refused when acting on the Queen's authority. 'I don't think you understand. Her Majesty has commanded that you put these on.'

'Tell her Majesty I refuse. She can put them on herself for all I care. We're facing doom! Don't you know that it's a day of doom!'

The girl was now more confused than appalled. 'I have no idea what you mean, but I'm certain that this will most displease Her Majesty!' And, with that, she picked up the bag and walked off in a fluster. Mordecai continued to sit in the dirt. Where else was he going to go that evening? Drink at Babak's? Hang out at Jere's for a laugh? Make himself a meal at home? No, here, weeping at the gates of the power that I've served faithfully for a decade is where I belong. There's a time

The Girl and the Guardian

for men to stand firm and there's a time for men to fall and weep before Heaven.

***

The servant returned to find the Queen anxiously waiting. 'Sorry your highness, but he won't accept the clothes. He said we're facing a day of doom.'

'"Doom"? What's he talking about?'

'I don't know. He wouldn't tell me.'

Esther was now concerned enough to take a risk. She sent her servant to summon a messenger she had come to respect. Usually, her female servants served her well. Now, however, she needed someone strong who could get answers out of Mordecai.

Hathach bowed as he entered the room. 'Yes, Your Majesty. You called for me?'

'I have an important job that needs doing.'

'I'm at your service, Your Majesty.'

'It's a highly confidential job. No one must know about it on pain of death,' Esther said with as much intimidation as she could muster in her eyes.

'As Your Majesty wishes,' Hathach replied. He was no young slave girl taken from the country. Hathach had grown up in the palace, and no one easily intimidated him. He understood that royalty had secrets that needed keeping. He knew that whenever they began speaking about 'pain of death this' or 'on your life that', it usually meant they were feeling insecure.

Esther went on to explain that Mordecai was a relative but that, for reasons she can't explain right now, he needed to guard this information. 'I'm entrusting you with the mission of finding out why my relative, a respected Persian administrator, is wailing in sackcloth and ashes in the streets.'

'I will do as you ask, Your Majesty,' Hathach said, bowing and turning to leave.

'Hatach!'

'Yes, Your Majesty?'

'Endeavor to find out all you can. When you speak to him, refer to me as "Hadassah".'

'As you wish.'

***

A big pair of feet stood in front of Mordecai. It's not the servant girl. Is it the guards to carry me away? He then looked up to see the face of a beardless man.

The Girl and the Guardian

43

'ARE YOU HERE to drop off clothes as well?' Mordecai said, looking up at the eunuch.

'The palace sent me to inquire about your condition, Mordecai.'

'How does my condition look?'

'Like crap. Like crap after a night of heavy drinking. Actually, the resemblance is uncanny.'

'It was more of a rhetorical question.'

'Listen, sir. My name's Hathach, and I need to have a big boy conversation with you on behalf of our mutual friend.'

'Did she send you with instructions to see me dressed properly?' Mordecai asked with an edge in his voice.

'We're talking about Hadassah, right?'

Hadassah? Mordecai noted the use of her Hebrew name. 'I see you're someone the Queen trusts. You have my attention.'

'The Queen is concerned for you as her relative. She wants to know what exactly it is that you're doing.'

'I'm fasting. And praying.'

'You're going without food?'

The Oliver Anderson Trilogy

'That's generally what people mean by the word. Ever tried it?'

'The Mages I serve sometimes do it for magical insight. But I'm a eunuch, and it's not really something we do.'

'Why not?'

'We don't get to have sex. So, we tend to focus heavily on our other appetite: food. This world may have taken my penis away, but there's no way they'll be taking my lunch,' Hathach said with a grin.

'I'm sorry I asked. I can't say I've ever considered the matter.'

'Glad I could enlighten you.'

'Well, oh great lover of lunches, now that you know I'm fasting, will there be anything else?'

'Yes. Why? The Queen doesn't understand why you are acting this way.'

'Not understand? How can she not? Has she lost her royal marbles?!'

'You're either brave or foolish to be speaking in annoyed tones about the Empress. I don't know your family history, but I've observed the girl's character. She doesn't deserve your criticism. She is wise beyond her years.'

'Is it wise to care about clothes and image when death is in the air?'

Hathach shook his head and clenched his fists. 'Can you hear?! Because right now, I think your ears would be better off turning into arseholes and dumping all over your shoulders.'

'Lovely thought.'

The Girl and the Guardian

'Oh, believe me, I have plenty more! Now, I need you to tell me why you're crying and wearing sackcloth because the Queen doesn't know. Fortunately for you, you're some sort of relative that she seems to care about. If you weren't, I'd have you thrown into a rat's toilet of a prison.'

It was then that the light clicked for Mordecai. 'You mean, she really doesn't know?' It hadn't occurred to Mordecai that a royal edict concerning the Jews could have come from the palace, sealed with her husband's ring, and Esther not be aware of it.

'You're not from the clever side of the family, are you? This is what I've been trying to say. Now, what is it that she doesn't know, but you obviously do?'

Mordecai calmed himself by taking a deep breath. 'Can't you hear the weeping that echoes through the streets of this blood-stained city?'

'I have only now left the palace,' he said before stopping to pause. 'Yes, now that I listen, I do hear a distant wailing.'

'It's the cry of a people facing their doom at the hands of the government.'

'Doom?'

'Yes, they've handed my people over to destruction.'

'Hmm. I've heard rumours in the palace. Supposedly the Viceroy issued a severe pronouncement against a group within the Empire this afternoon. But I'm ignorant of the details.'

'I'll give you a hint. The commotion you hear? It's coming from the Jewish quarter.'

'The Jewish quarter? But that would mean that you're—'

'Yes, I am.'

'But then, that would also mean the Queen—'

'Yes, she is.'

Hathach had seen much in his palace career—it had been a while since anything had stunned him. *That explains her Star Maker*, he thought.

Mordecai handed Hathach the parchment. 'She isn't aware of the edict. Take it. I took this only hours ago. Read it yourself if you wish. But please, show it to the Queen. Tell her that her people need her. If she doesn't intercede before the Emperor, we're finished. Tell her that Haman is an Agagite. She'll understand what that means.'

The Girl and the Guardian

44

HORROR FILLED ESTHER'S chest like wet clay as she read the letter. Her mind raced to take it all in. She asked Hathach to tell her all that Mordecai had said, having dismissed all servants except him.

My husband is going to murder me. The thought burned through her mind. *An Agagite? Really? I knew he wasn't Persian, but the sworn enemy of our people? Foolish girl! Naïve girl! Heaven makes you the Queen, and you're not even aware the Viceroy is an Agagite?*

Esther knew that scolding herself wasn't going to help. What could she do? They banished Vashti for refusing an oral command—how then could she challenge a written one sealed with the Imperial ring? She knew that, unlike other wives, she didn't have the luxury of going to her husband whenever she wanted. Xerxes wasn't merely a husband; he was the Emperor. No one came before him uninvited. She'd seen those axe-wielding bodyguards and didn't want to test the limits. The edict terrified her, but what could she do?

The Oliver Anderson Trilogy

The fear of going uninvited before the King cut deeper than any sword. Helplessness engulfed her. She sent Hathach back to her cousin with her reply: *You know the law about approaching the Emperor. He hasn't called me for over a month. There's nothing I can do.*

Mordecai received the message. For a moment, his heart stopped aching for the Jewish nation. Instead, his heart turned its concern towards that awkward and chubby nine-year-old girl he had raised and mentored. He knew she was afraid. He knew she wanted to hide like a child behind her royal crown. An urge rose within him to be with her and hold her hand. He longed to look her in the eye and tell her, as he had done so many times growing up, not to be afraid. He wanted to remind her that Heaven was with her, that she could stand firm, and that she had a job to do. What could he say through this eunuch that would remind her of everything he had tried to teach her?

Hathach came back with the message:

Don't trust your crown to save you, child. If you choose to give in to fear and do nothing, Heaven will rescue our people. But you will have missed out and will perish under the regret. Think: why did Heaven make you, a Jewish commoner, Queen over this pagan Empire? Why did Heaven make you beautiful? To serve yourself? No. You are not some victim of peculiar events. Consider that Heaven brought you here for this very moment of deliverance.

***

The Girl and the Guardian

Esther had Hathach repeat it. It was as if Mordecai was there in the room with her. He had often told her that Jews were not victims. Were they oppressed at times? Yes. But victims? Never. They were Heaven's people. And Heaven's people walk with gratitude and dignity. *Because he has set his love on me, therefore I will deliver him. I will set him on high, because he knows my name*, she whispered from Psalm 91. She didn't need to be afraid of losing anything. Not really. Her beauty and privilege were not something she had earned. They were temporary gifts to be used to serve Heaven.

Hatach stood at attention, awaiting her reaction. She took a deep breath. 'If I can't risk losing my influence, then Persia has devoured me, and I'm its slave. This palace won't own me, and this crown won't define me!'

Hathach smiled. 'You are the wisest queen I've ever had the honour to serve. Your Star-Maker favours you.'

Esther smiled and hoped he was right. 'Here's the message you're to give Mordecai,

Get everyone to do a three-day, dry fast.
This will need a miracle! I'll go uninvited before the Emperor,
hoping he won't be angry. And, if I die trying to save my
people, so be it.

Mordecai got the message and whispered towards heaven. 'That's my girl.'

189

45

OLIVER RAISED HIS hand. William nodded. 'Aye.'

'The fasting I know about helps you lose weight and get healthy. But what's fasting like for Jews and Christians? What does Esther mean by a "dry" fast?'

'Love that yer asking about fastin'—immediately after a big lunch. Doesn't seem quite so intimidatin'!'

'Not my fault. Esther started it.'

'How about we go for a walk—a bit of breeze and scenery might do wonders for a Londoner. Ye'll see lots of green stuff on the ground. Around here, we call it grass. It won't hurt ye. Our cows and sheep eat it and turn it into meat. Magic, really.'

'Funny. London does have parks, you know.'

'Ye spend much time in 'em?'

'Not as much as I should. But, yes. A walk sounds good. I'll get my shoes.'

'Here, take these instead.' William reached down and grabbed a pair of rubber wellies and handed them over to Oliver. 'We won't be walkin' on paved roads, and the grass is tall.'

The Girl and the Guardian

'Gotcha.'

***

The two Andersons exited the old cabin and began their trek over and around the windswept hills that surrounded it. Oliver walked daily through the streets of London—but this seemed more like a hike than a walk.

'Typically fastin' is when ye go without eatin' for a certain period. Ye drink water and the digestive system goes to sleep. Yer body then uses its stored energy—body fat—as fuel. If ye do it properly, it produces mental clarity.'

'Is the mental clarity for prayer?'

'That's part of it, yes. Now dry fastin' is a different beast. It's when ye go without water as well as food. I don't recommend that one, laddie—it leaves ye weakened and desperate! Regular fastin' can be healthy and leave you feeling and looking better. But a dry fast dehydrates ye and leaves ye feeling and looking rough.'

'That's nuts! Why would anyone do that to themselves?'

'The Bible only mentions dry fastin' a couple of times, and it was when people were in life or death emergencies. It's a radically humblin' act. Yet it's what Hadassah does and what she calls the Jews to do with her. Through this fast, God is changin' Esther. He is emptyin' her of all the bits of Vashti that still live within her.'

'Does this increase her spiritual beauty?'

'Good question! I'd say it makes her trust more in God's beauty, not her own. So, in a sense, yes. Martin Luther said somethin' along these lines—'

'Martin Luther, the civil rights guy?'

'No. This was the original Luther, the Protestant Reformer. The civil rights guy was named after him. The original Luther said, "Whoever makes himself beautiful, is made ugly. On the contrary, he who makes himself ugly is made beautiful." That's how things work in God's Kingdom.'

'Sounds like an upside-down kingdom.'

'Ye might say that. Esther is trustin' God for the beauty she'll be wearing when she goes before Xerxes' throne. She won't be placing confidence in herself.'

'Is that what believers do? You have faith instead of confidence? That's one reason I hesitate to look into religion.' Oliver struggled to get more than a couple of sentences out at a time. Keeping up with his grandfather's brisk pace up the hills was leaving him breathless. 'I think it's important to have confidence. If you're beautiful or smart or gifted, what's wrong with being confident in it?'

'Yer question shows that ye misunderstand both faith and human nature. It's not wrong to be confident. That's what faith is all about,' he said with something akin to a shout as they reached the top of the hill. 'The word "confident" comes from the Latin *con* and *fide,* which means "with faith". We all have faith. Some have faith in God. Some put faith in a relationship, a career, their intelligence, or beauty."

The Girl and the Guardian

Oliver stood next to his grandfather and began to survey the magnificent Highland view. 'So it's not wrong to be confident?'

William clamped a hand on his grandson's shoulder. 'Not a bit. Faith in God realises that this life has problems that are too big for ye. When ye face these giants with confidence in yer own strength instead of God's, yer actin' in arrogance and settin' yerself up for failure. Esther knows her life and her nation is at stake. She needs more than human attractiveness to rescue it.'

'Gotcha. So, what happens?'

William pulled a flask from his trousers. He took a swig and handed it to his grandson. 'Have that wee dram we were talkin' about earlier. You drink, I'll talk.'

46

THESE CLOTHES AREN'T me, not today, she thought.

After three days of fasting, the Queen felt like wearing sackcloth and ashes, not a royal robe. Her body was weary, and her soul was humbled. She was sorry for her own sins and the sins of her people. She confessed her fears, her bitterness towards Xerxes, her pride in appearance, and her anger towards Heaven for ripping her Jewish life from her. The insidious voice that tempted her to hide her ethnicity and save herself was now only a distant whisper. Instead of clinging to the safety of her quarters, she would make a dangerous attempt to approach the King uninvited.

In this regard, Xerxes manifested a common human paradox: the more out of control his inner life got, the more he wanted regulation in the world around him. There had, of course, been some genuine assassination attempts on his life. Xerxes had two axe wielders on either side of him whenever he left his personal quarters. If any uninvited person approached the King, they were to be hacked to pieces. Their only hope was if Xerxes held out his sceptre, thereby extending a gracious welcome.

The Girl and the Guardian

Approaching Xerxes uninvited could easily be misunderstood as rebellion, and Esther needed more than her own beauty or charm to get her through.

She waited in the courtyard. *Shouldn't I be feeling some chutzpah by now?* Her heart hammered as she faced the entrance to the throne room. She felt zero courage. The doors were still closed. *What if he's in a bad mood when they open? I could face banishment, like Vashti—or, maybe worse.* Her weakened knees began to knock. *Should I turn back? Someone help me!*

Suddenly, she saw an unexpected face approaching her from the left. 'Hathach?'

'Your Majesty, may I speak with you for just a moment.'

'I am hoping to see the King. I know you're probably aware of that.'

'I am, Your Majesty. That is why I wanted to speak to you. I will be brief.'

'Please, proceed.'

'I have been musing over the secrets you and Mordecai shared with me as messenger a few days ago. It has brought something to my remembrance.'

Esther nodded. 'Go ahead.'

'I believe the stars are in your favour, Your Majesty.'

'That's kind of you to say, Hathach.'

'Wait, please. I know it is not your habit to look to stars for guidance, but I speak about something that was given to my order by one who was both one of you and one of me.'

195

'What are you speaking about, Hathach? This sounds like riddles.'

'I speak of Daniel, your prophet, and the man who was head of our order two generations ago.'

Esther's eyes widened. 'Yes, of course, all Jews know about Daniel! But what does he have to do with me?'

'Before he died, he left a prophecy for our order—one he had written through the power of your Hebrew magic. I believe that you are destined to fulfil this prophecy.'

Esther shook her head. Her jaw dropped. 'I'm, I'm... what?' she stuttered, fighting to understand what Hathach was saying.

'It would take too long to explain it all now, Your Majesty. But I wanted to encourage you: you will defeat the dragon! It is your destiny.'

And with that, Hathach bowed, turned, and left Esther simultaneously encouraged and confused. Usually, she wouldn't pay any attention to the astrological words of the Magi. But the name of Daniel shook her. *Was this a sign from Heaven?* Whether it was or not, she suddenly felt courage where previously there was none.

As she stood there musing, the doors opened, and from within the throne room, Xerxes glanced toward the courtyard. An unexpected image attracted Xerxes' attention. Into his day of wearisome politics, his young bride appeared in regal attire. The nineteen-year-old Empress with raven's hair, olive skin, and midnight eyes walked towards him haloed with the golden, jewel-studded tiara he had personally overseen the fashioning

The Girl and the Guardian

of. Her lips were rich and soft, and her purple gown draped over a figure that was both sensual and noble.

Yet it wasn't only her ripened physical beauty—unrivalled as it was. Xerxes was used to having the world's most beautiful women. It was her demeanour. There was a look in her eyes as she approached him that wouldn't let him turn away. It was the rare look of a woman possessing complete confidence but without a trace of arrogance. She flowed across the throne room like a liquid sonnet while the hem of her robe whispered upon the marble floor. She clasped her hands together beneath her breasts in a self-possessed modesty that was foreign to the flaunting culture of the Persian court. It was femininity—as poetic as it was pure.

Esther approached the one who had kidnapped and forced her into marriage—only to desert her for his harem. The Queen then bowed. The King extended his sceptre, and the guards lowered their axes.

'Hello, my Queen.' He noticed a tremor run down her body. 'Are you okay? If you need anything, ask, and I'll empty half the Kingdom.'

Esther smiled back, grateful both that her head was still on her shoulders and that her husband had so warmly welcomed her. She proceeded with the strategy. 'I've prepared a wine banquet along with some of your favourite foods, Your Majesty. Please grant me the honour of feasting with me today. And, as he is your chief minister, bring Haman for your company, if you so please.'

197

Xerxes had a reputation for unpredictability, but Esther wasn't clueless. She had learned her husband's tastes. For Xerxes, there was no such thing as bad wine. There was only some wine that wasn't as good as other wine.

His eyes lit up. 'I'd love to! Whatever you desire, you can ask me then.'

'I am most grateful, Your Majesty.'

He turned to a messenger. 'Find Haman and relay Queen Esther's request.'

The Girl and the Guardian

47

THE LIQUID WARMTH, the magnificent view, and the short rest revitalised Oliver. 'Keep on walking?' he asked with fresh confidence.

'Can you keep up with me, laddie?'

'The English aren't all as soft as you Scots like to think.'

'Glad to hear you say it. Now demonstrate it!' And off William darted at a pace even quicker than before.

'It sounds like there may be hope for Esther's marriage, after all,' Oliver said, determined to keep stride with his grandfather.

'Aye. It was a lovely welcome. But Esther probably attributed that more to Heaven's favour than to any lastin' change in her husband or marriage.'

'Before lunch, you talked about how sex in marriage was good. You said it was key for family life and children. But all that only pushes the "why" question back. Why a mum and a dad? Why weddings?'

'Yer askin' some deep questions.'

'They too much for you, Gandalf?'

The Oliver Anderson Trilogy

'Watch it, laddie. I keep my beard better trimmed than him.' William reflected as Oliver kept up with his brisk stride. He appreciated his grandson's curiosity and hoped to communicate what he knew in a way that made sense to the young man. 'In the Bible, God presents himself as a husband to his people. When he does so, he's not spontaneously choosin' a metaphor. He didn't think, "Let me see, how can I best explain my plans? I know, marriage! They're into that!" No. God's purpose for sex and marriage stretches from Eden's first sunrise to the world's last night. He had planned to redeem a people for Himself from the beginning. For that reason, he created marriage as a sacrament.'

'A sacrament?' Oliver asked, determined to keep up with his grandfather this time. 'Isn't that a Catholic thing?'

'I'm as Baptist as they get, laddie. But the word "sacrament" isn't a bad one. Give those Papists their due when they deserve it. It means that marriage is a picture, a symbol of something greater than itself—somethin' that God is doing.'

'What's marriage supposed to be a picture of?'

'God gave us weddin's so that we could look forward to the great, eternal weddin'. That's when we'll forget all our faults and sorrows and the endless party will begin. God also gave us sex so that marital love could be faithful, intense, and fruitful.'

'I get that. But why?'

'Why? Because all three of these characteristics describe God's love for us. As in marriage, God faithfully loves us. He doesn't get bored and move on to a believer who is more

The Girl and the Guardian

interestin' than ye. Also, sex is intense. That's how God loves ye—with intensity. It's not an emotionally detached love. God's love for you has passion and desire. Marital sex is also fruitful—and so is God's love. It causes ye to be born again.'

'That phrase, "born-again", doesn't it describe Christians that are a bit too enthusiastic?'

'The centre of the Christian message is that ye need a new life. This is why sex and marriage are essential practices for us to get right. As the husband enters into the woman to release his seed and brings life, so God sends His Word, Christ, into humanity so that we can be born anew. That may sound weird to yer ears, but it's a key teachin' of the New Testament. St. Peter wrote, "For ye have been born again, not of seed that perishes, but of seed that never perishes—through God's livin' and endurin' word". Does that make any sense to ye?'

'It sounds weird. I don't know why. I'm used to thinking of sex as something dirty and unrelated to God. It makes sense. But this puts us in the position of the woman, doesn't it?'

'Yes, it does. CS Lewis said something to that effect.'

Oliver grinned. 'Is that you citing an Englishman as an authority?'

William grinned back. 'Lewis was Northern Irish. Much more tolerable.'

'I thought I had you!'

'Lewis, in thinking about the symbolism behind gender, said that humanity is the feminine before God who's the masculine.'

'Is that sexist?'

'There ye are again. I dunno. Is biology sexist? All he means is that God comes into this world to impregnate it with new life. This is why Scriptures always refer to God as the great Husband of Israel or the church. Never the 'spouse' or the 'wife'. Gender and sexuality play critical roles in revealin' the mystery of God. Biology is not completely separate from theology.'

Oliver was beginning to lose stride. 'Grandpa.'

'Aye?'

'Another flask break?'

'Of course.'

'I think my script needs this.'

'Scotch?'

'No,' Oliver laughed in reply. 'It needs more depth—symbols maybe. I'm not sure. What I'm trying to write seems shallow; like I'm writing about nothing. Esther and Mordecai, they believed in something bigger than themselves. They lived with purpose, with meaning.'

William took a swig then handed the flask to his grandson. 'The story's not over yet. Ye'll find yer inspiration before the end.'

The Girl and the Guardian

48

'TRY THIS WINE next, my dear Haman,' Esther said with a coy smile and batting eyelashes. Haman enjoyed the company of a beautiful woman as much as the next man, but he knew that this was no mere woman. She was the Empress, the most desirable woman in the world. This was the longest he had ever been in her presence, and he found both her beauty and charm exhilarating. Her eyes and wine invited his words—and they flowed out of him like a bubbling brook.

'The food and wine are almost as splendid as yourself, Your Majesty.'

'Thank you, Viceroy. I hear that you are bringing justice and much needed reform to our capital. Please, tell me more about your vision.'

Haman was a scrupulous man with strong feelings about right and wrong. He'd always been faithful to his wife, Zeresh. He was proud of his morality, but this meal was stroking that same pride in another direction. The most beautiful women in the world, the Queen over all queens, was here in his presence,

The Oliver Anderson Trilogy

praising his accomplishments. After three glasses of wine, the man who usually didn't flirt was finding it hard not to.

The fact that he was also in the presence of the King of kings helped his self-control tremendously. Xerxes had given Haman his authority. But this authority did not extend to his wife or his concubines. Xerxes, like most men, preferred to keep his women to himself. All around the room, the King's Immortal bodyguards stood, always ready to kill on the King's command. Haman was hoping they weren't gazing at him too closely as he adjusted his seating posture to hide potential evidence that he was enjoying the Queen's company more than he should.

I'm charming the most beautiful woman in the world. And why not? She might not be used to men who had to work their way to the top. Haman believed he was captivating the beauty of all beauties. He would never touch another man's wife. That would violate his moral code. Xerxes did such things, and he believed, deep down, that he was a better man than the debauched King that he served. But he didn't mind relishing in Esther's attention. *After all, I've acted justly. I deserve this as a reward.* Haman loved himself—and loving himself was something he was good at.

Haman was acting exactly as Esther had hoped. She wasn't flirting; not overtly. But she was making space for him to flirt. The words of her pleasantries and polite conversation could not be faulted. But, in the shadow of those innocent words, her eyes shot him glances.

This was her trap.

The Girl and the Guardian

Esther didn't enjoy Haman's company. Far from it. She would have preferred wallowing in pig filth. But there was a method to her madness. She found the strength to persevere through the meal from the Psalm of David: *You prepare a table before me in the presence of my enemies.* And, in the power of her faith, she let her eyes smile, and her words be few and lovely.

Xerxes smiled at Esther. 'My love, you've outdone yourself. The meal is perfect.' The King was delighted. He was familiar with beautiful yet proud queens who tried to push their independent power. He also knew concubines who used their sexual prowess to seduce, manipulate, and win favours. But Esther's femininity was different. It was subtle and charming. He knew she wanted something, but she wasn't bullying to obtain it. Whenever she spoke to him, he felt respected.

He was encountering a form of femininity that was rare in his circles—and it was conquering him. It was a sexual love—how could he not think in sexual terms when it came to a woman as beautiful as Esther?—but it was somehow different to the sexual pleasure he experienced in the harem. Eyeing his wife and remembering her naked body in all its perfection, stirred a healthy desire within him. This was his wife—and the desires to protect and provide rose up within him.

Not that the King was fully conscious of all this. Self-awareness was not one of his qualities. He was enjoying the food and wine, and, when he finished those, he stabbed a

205

hookah pipe in his mouth. It was a great meal and, if the King had any regret, it was that he brought Haman along. He usually enjoyed drinks with Haman. Technically, Haman was his slave. But he was also the closest thing he had to a friend—if divine emperors can have friends. Haman's conversation and insights were usually valued. But, here at Queen Esther's magnificent banquet, he felt uneasy. It was only a half-formed thought—he was too busy eating, drinking, and undressing Esther with his eyes for any deep thinking—but the feeling was somewhere in the background. He was vaguely aware that his chief minister was directing much of his conversation towards his Queen—and perhaps enjoying it more than he should.

As he did earlier in the throne room, the King looked at Esther and said, 'Ask for anything, and I'll give it to you!'

Esther bowed low to her King. 'If I have pleased you, then let me prepare another banquet for Haman and you tomorrow. Then I'll let you know my petition.'

'Of course, my love,' he said—the words leaping out.

'I shall look forward to it with great anticipation, Your Highness,' Haman said with a smile and a bow.

Without wasting any time, Esther rose, cast a final smile at the King and Haman, and then left the room.

The King was happy and curiously eager for tomorrow. Yet an unease stirred. *Today's banquet was in my honour, with Haman as my chosen guest. Tomorrow it's 'for Haman and you'?* Esther's behaviour had been far too modest for anyone to find fault with. But Haman? He had not been so subtle.

206

49

OLIVER SHOOK HIS head. 'What a crazy situation for Esther to be in. And I thought my scriptwriting was stressing me out!'

'Ready to begin walkin' again?'

'Definitely. Think you can keep up, old man?'

'Old man? Laddie, I'm in my prime!' he shouted.

'Wait! No cheating!'

And off they went as Lords of the land—exuding mirth with every leap and bound that they took. It was clear that William knew every hill, stream, and flower patch. This was his land—and the surroundings reflected his rugged sweetness.

'Getting any ideas for yer script?'

'How about aliens?'

William laughed. 'That's desperate! Perhaps ye can even have one 'em tryin' to phone home. How ye findin' our Bible story.'

'There's drama! I can't believe Esther managed to keep her cool in Haman's presence like that. Talk about pressure! I'm not sure I could handle that—theatre school is tough enough. I'm curious though, are all the Bible's stories like this?'

207

'All its stories are unique. But ye might be surprised what's in the Bible if ye gave it a closer look.'

'Does it say anything about stress?'

'St. Paul wrote to the church in Phillipi, "The Lord is near. Don't be anxious, but in everythin', let your requests be known to God. Pray and give thanks. And God's peace, that passes understandin', will rule your hearts." How's that?'

Oliver looked over at his grandfather as they kept up their brisk pace. 'It's pretty, but it sounds trite.'

'How so?'

'Anxiety can be caused by several factors, right?'

'Sure, lot's of things can provoke it: poor diet, not enough sleep, drinking weird caramel latte things—'

'They're not that bad.'

'In that verse, Paul gives us three truths to help us keep our peace. First, he tells us to pray. Yes, he knows yer needs and all the details, but He wants to hear ye talk about it anyway.'

'So prayer is kinda like a mindfulness app?'

'Like a what-nap?'

'It's a... nevermind.'

'Secondly, he tells ye to give thanks. Givin' thanks is more than a quick, token prayer we say before eatin' our food. True gratitude is the way we should see the world. God's a continual giver, and we're continual receivers of His gifts.'

'I can see how that works. If you believe that God is in control, that he's good, and that everything in your life is a gift from him—I can see how that would help you relax.'

208

The Girl and the Guardian

'Yer not as thick as ye look.'

'Thanks?'

'Lastly, it says, 'The Lord is near.' That's important for ye to remember. Sometimes circumstances hide God. Esther may have wondered if her participation in this contest or her distance from Jerusalem would have kept God from hearin' her prayers, yet we see Him with her. Ye may not always hear God speakin' clearly. Yet, because of Jesus, we can be sure that He's near. Like Esther, ye might be in situations where you feel face to face with yer enemy or even with death itself. But God's nearness is something ye never have to doubt.'

'If your cask doesn't relax me this evening, who knows, I may be desperate enough to go for a God-fix.'

'Don't be sarky.'

'Sorry. How about coffee when we get back?'

'Is the black stuff growing on ye?'

'Maybe,' Oliver reluctantly admitted. 'Well, what happens with Esther and the King? I'm not sure I understand where Esther is taking this meal thing—but it seems she has a strategy and is keeping to it.'

'Aye. She's bein' strategic. You want me to continue?'

Oliver nodded but, as he was breathing harder than usual, it took a moment for sound to come out. 'Yes. Please.'

The Oliver Anderson Trilogy

50

MORDECAI VENTURED BACK to the office after four days of absence. He had sent word to his assistants that he was sick and to manage without him. They knew, of course, why he hadn't come in. They had been present when the messenger read the proclamation. During this time, Mordecai had joined with other Jews in humbling themselves in fasting, prayer, and confession in hopes that Heaven's King would see fit to overrule what the Persian throne had pronounced against them.

He walked towards the gates and looked over to where he had sat in sackcloth a few days earlier. It was surreal to enter the headquarters of the institution that was determined to kill you. But Mordecai, dutiful to the end, felt obliged to give his workers some direction. Besides, what was he to do for the next few months? Sit at home and wait for the scheduled day of death to arrive? Mordecai couldn't stomach the thought of such inaction.

A shout tore through his musings. 'Make way!' Mordecai looked up. Someone important was headed in his direction.

It can't be! Haman had finished his afternoon meal with the royals and was headed home. The soldiers and other passers-by bowed as his horse approached the gate while Mordecai stood in disbelief. He wasn't hard to spot, and Haman smiled at the sight of him. Defeat had smeared itself all over Mordecai's face.

Haman called out. 'Are you alright, servant? Don't you know enough to bow before your Viceroy? A man in your position shouldn't be so ignorant of the protocol.'

Mordecai barely registered his words as the horror of the situation bludgeoned his senses. He lowered his eyes and opened his mouth to say something diplomatic, trying and avoid the painful insanity of the confrontation, but no words came out. Every thought that raced through his mind seemed foolish. Here he was, a son of Israel, a Benjaminite, and a descendant of King Saul himself—altogether powerless before an Agag of Amalek. *Beg. Plead for his forgiveness,* the voice of self-preservation rang through his head. *Maybe, even now, you can make peace.*

Haman saw the desperation in Mordecai's eyes and began to mock. 'You look lost. Has something tragic happened? Have you received some bit of bad news?' Haman laughed—still half-drunk with wine and thoroughly enjoying the moment. 'Justice is finally coming!'

Justice? Is that what he thinks this is? Mordecai objected to Haman's words, but he trembled before this man with near limitless authority.

The Viceroy's scorn thickened. 'The destruction your people dished out to other nations, nations more worthy than yours, is coming back to haunt you. Now it's you who have been weighed in the scales and found wanting. Soon the earth will no longer have to bear the injustice of the Jewish insect.'

Mordecai felt the need to say something. 'I…I…There's no…' and he lowered his head again, unable to form a complete phrase or sentence as terror washed over him. He had been stricken dumb in the face of such total power and absolute hatred and struggled even to draw his breath.

Haman laughed at Mordecai's speechlessness. 'Servant, today is your lucky day. I've eaten and am in good spirits. How would you like to receive mercy?' Mordecai looked back up, mouth open, with confusion in his eyes.

'That's right. I'm prepared to throw a crumb from my table. Would you like some mercy? If you bow to me now, before this crowd, then on the thirteenth day of Adar, I'll see that you're spared. I'll grant your life, and you can serve me to old age. How does that sound? Decide. I may not feel so charitable tomorrow.'

Is he really offering me my life? Mordecai looked around him at the others who were prostrate before Haman. He hadn't even realised he was still standing. The unexpected encounter had frozen him in his place. His heart raced, and a desperation to live pulsed through him. The immense intimidation weighed heavy on his shoulders and weakened his knees. The darkness was overwhelming him.

The Girl and the Guardian

'It won't be long until the name of Israel is only a distant memory. Look at me, Jew! Look at the one who will erase your name from under Heaven. What good will all your standing have done then? Nothing. Do yourself a favour. Save your skin. Bow. I'll accept a mere kneel. Can you kneel, Mordecai?'

A kneel? The possibility raced through Mordecai's mind. *I can do a kneel. Nothing's wrong with a kneel. Is there?* Mordecai couldn't think of any clear commandment from Moses that should keep him from kneeling before a civil leader. But he knew it would be wrong to save his own skin while his people died. *You've been kneeling your whole life to try and make this work,* a voice rang out in his soul. Whether the idea was of his own thinking or of Heaven, he didn't know. But he knew the ring of truth when he heard it. He had wanted so bad to be both a model Hebrew and an exemplary Persian that he had often played both sides and been overly compliant.

'What will it be, Mordecai?' Haman asked with a wide grin. 'I give glory to servants who honour me. Be a good Persian. Kneel.'

Just when Mordecai thought he no longer had the strength to stand, a shaft of light stabbed through his fear. A word about standing flashed before his mind. He had been in the synagogue the day before, praying with the Jews, when someone had read out 'For I know that my rescuer lives, and he will stand on the earth.' It was a verse from Job—a man who had stared into destruction's eyeballs.

The thought infused Mordecai with strength, and he raised his eyes to meet the Viceroy. 'Thank you for your offer, Your Excellency, but no thank you. We have a Rescuer,' he said, surprised at the boldness of his words as please-don't-kill-me-now adrenaline pumped through him.

Haman looked down at a new set of eyes, ones that gazed back at him with courage and confidence. 'You won't bow?'

Mordecai held the Viceroy's gaze and as courage grew within him. 'Even when we are too weak to stand, our Rescuer does. He will stand with us today—and on the thirteenth of Adar.'

Haman's rage erupted within him. 'Insolent Jew!'

Mordecai looked into Haman's eyes and confronted him with the truth of the situation. 'I do not work against your authority, yet you seek to kill my people and me. You are the Viceroy, and I respect the law. But, given your evil intentions, I will not bow to you, even if it would save my life,' Mordecai proclaimed with increased volume. 'I stand before you—I can do no other. May Heaven look after it's people and deliver us from your evil.' With that, Mordecai turned, walked past the Viceroy, and into the citadel.

Haman's royal meal had inflated his ego. But being talked back to by an emboldened Mordecai popped that same ego like a needle on a balloon. He bit his elite tongue, fighting to maintain his self-control. *Don't yell, you're above him. He will suffer soon enough.* He turned his head and rode forward, trying to seem as self-composed as Mordecai.

51

BY THE TIME he arrived home, Haman was in a foul spirit. Zeresh greeted him at the door. 'Good to see you, darling. I expected you home an hour ago. Our friends will be here shortly.'

'Tonight?' Haman's mind was, by this point, half-a-world away from the social plans his wife had laid for them. 'Ah, that's right. I'd forgotten—my day had some twists. I'll get dressed and be right down.'

His wife shook her head and sighed. 'Ah, men.'

Haman called his servant and headed upstairs to his room. Getting his Viceroy robes off and into proper dinner attire was no small feat. He looked forward to the evening. These weren't fake, political friends coming over, they were the real deal. He would be able to unload on them the glory of his time with the Queen and the continued insolence that was Mordecai. They'd understand.

As Haman relished his second luxurious meal of the day, he recounted everything to his wife and friends. 'I've all a man could wish for. Power! Money! My wife and I have a good

215

marriage. Now I have the favour of the Queen and the King. I've ten sons who share my values and work with me. I should walk with my head held high. But I can't enjoy any of it as long as that filthy piece of donkey vomit disrespects me so openly.'

Zeresh looked sympathetically towards her husband. 'My poor dear. It's upsetting to have someone not treat you the way you deserve. Can't you eliminate him? Even if Mordecai is a royal official, wouldn't Xerxes permit you to terminate him?'

Haman had expected to dispose of Mordecai on the big day—but why not make an early example of him? He nodded. 'Perhaps.'

Their friends shook their heads. 'As a Persian, I find this so embarrassing. Your family came to Susa as immigrants, and you worked your way up to where you are. Some Persians can't stand an outsider being successful. Is that it, do you think? That this man disrespects you for being a foreigner?'

'Being an Amalekite has something to do with it.'

'We Persians like to think of ourselves as enlightened. It appals me that some treat non-Persians this way.'

Zeresh's anger pushed her to stand straight up. 'Why not make an example of him? Have him impaled?!! It would send a clear message to everyone that we'll not tolerate this in Persia.'

'Yes!' the friends cheered. 'Persia cannot know peace if it does not also know justice. You should not be treated this way.'

Their words stroked Haman's ego like a kitten. Mordecai had continued to disrespect him—even after the death edict. Why not ask the King for permission to kill him immediately? If he banished Vashti for insubordination, executing a royal official for the same offence wouldn't be unimaginable.

'You're right,' he said, looking across the table to his friends. 'I'll make the request to the King in the morning. Then I'll enjoy my afternoon meal at the palace without any distraction.'

'Wonderful! Do it!' his friends affirmed.

Haman raised his voice. 'Servants!'

Immediately, three young men rushed into the room and bowed. 'Yes, Your Excellence.'

'Erect an execution pole. Make it huge—seventy-five feet high! And do it immediately.'

***

Haman's arm wrapped around Zeresh's waist like a birthday ribbon as they admired the massive woodwork in front of them. The clear moonlight illuminated the edifice, revealing its impressive height to the neighbourhood. Their friends had left an hour ago.

Zeresh took a sip of wine and lifted her lips to her husband's ear. 'I'm proud of you,' she whispered. Haman tingled with the warmth men experience when they achieve success at work, family, or, in his case, both. He hoped that his father and grandfather would've been proud of this project.

Three of their sons were also outside, admiring the height of the rapidly constructed pole. The rest were inside. All grown up, they shared his strength of vision.

The Oliver Anderson Trilogy

Haman kissed her gently. 'I need to get bed now. I'll sleep better now that we've mounted this properly.'

'Bed? It's such a beautiful moment,' Zeresh pleaded with a smile. 'But you're right. You have a big day coming. Hopefully, by this time tomorrow, we'll have impaled Mordecai on this spike, and his blood will be dripping before our feet.'

'I'm certain of it.' He kissed her back. 'Hire some musicians if you can. We'll make a party of it.'

'As you wish, darling.'

Haman turned and left her standing on their patio, went off to bed, and dreamt about killing all the Jews in Persia.

52

HAMAN SKIPPED OUT of bed the next morning. Self-confidence radiated from his face.

Today I eliminate a poisonous person from my life.
Not that it's not primarily about my honour. No, it's for the peace and justice of Persia.
And after I've seen to Mordecai, I'll have another banquet with the delicious Queen.

He splashed water on his faces, and his servants arrayed him in regal robes while one of them led his horse to the main entrance. Then off he went to work, earlier than usual, for what promised to be a day of glory.

***

At the palace, the King was also up early—but his spirits were not as elevated as Haman's. Something about the way his banquet with the Queen had played out haunted his sleep. In his dreams, a spectre of jealousy, a spirit largely unfamiliar to Xerxes, haunted him. He felt as if someone was stabbing him in the back. The King tossed and turned, but failed to find a deep and peaceful sleep. Finally, something like morning appeared, and he felt an unusual urge to dress and head early into court to see if any royal matters needed his attention.

***

'Jahan!'

The court scribe snapped to attention as the King bolted into the throne room. 'Yes, Your Majesty!'

'Is there anyone waiting in the outer court to see me?'

Jahan's mind raced to remember if anyone had called for an emergency meeting that might warrant the King's presence so early in the morning. He couldn't remember a thing. 'No, not at this hour, Your Majesty. No one is usually here before dawn.'

'Hmm. Well, if no one is here to see me, perhaps I should review the royal records.'

'Review the royal records, Your Majesty?' Jahan said with a mixture of disbelief and fear. Royals never performed such tedious tasks unless something was wrong—and certainly not the likes of Xerxes.

The King looked as his slave with annoyance. 'Yes, the records! And why not? I am King and Emperor. Shouldn't I know the state of my realm? '

'Yes, Your Majesty!'

'Why are you surprised?! Bring out the records from the last two years and read them to me.'

The Girl and the Guardian

'The last two years?!' Jahan exclaimed, wondering if he hadn't fallen asleep in the twilight hours and slipped into a dream. 'Yes, Your Majesty!' Jahan dashed to the records and returned, rolling a cart laden with thin, clay tablets. He set one up on the reading table and began to read for the King.

The sound of someone going on about the details of court life was what Xerxes needed. His mind focused on the sound of Jahan's voice. He rested his head back on his throne and slowly drifted into rest. Right as he was about to fall into his long-coveted sleep, however, Jahan read something that pierced right through the thick daze and stood before his conscious mind—something firm that he could not dismiss.

'Scribe!'

'Yes, Your Majesty. Go back and read that again.'

'Cucumber salad was prepared to go with the lamb on Monday—'

'No! The one before.'

'Apologies, Your Majesty. "Information regarding the treachery of Bigthan and Teresh came to us via Queen Esther. She later revealed that the source she relied on for the information was a certain Mordecai, a royal civil servant for the city of—"'

'Mordecai?' The King interrupted. 'I don't know the man. Do you?'

'I've not met him myself, Your Majesty. I believe he's one of our younger executives working for the city itself.'

'Did we reward him for passing on this information?'

The Oliver Anderson Trilogy

'No, Your Majesty. It seems we praised the Queen for unmasking the plot at the time. She only shared the identity of her source later.'

'The Queen confederated herself well—and probably honoured that servant. But a ruler who fails to reward those devoted to him shouldn't be surprised to see his friends shrink and his enemies increase. How should I—'

A guard cried out. 'Haman in the outer court!'

'Haman? Already? Let him in,' he commanded.

Haman scurried into the court and bowed before the King. 'Your Majesty, what a joy to see you. There is a small matter that I'd like to raise—'

'Haman, you're here early.' Haman was in such a happy mood that he didn't notice the King's cooler-than-usual tone. 'I was about to ask Jahan a question, but I'd like to hear your advice instead.'

Haman was delighted to be needed. 'As you wish, Your Majesty.'

'What is a way to give great honour to a man for service to the Crown?'

Haman's vanity danced wildly in his mind, but, on this occasion, it made a tragic misstep. *How would I like for the King to honour me?* Haman's pride mused. *I have everything a man could desire. I'm like the King—except that I lack a throne and a queen like Esther.*

Haman advised what his heart craved. 'Robe the man in one of your royal suits. Seat him on a royal horse and order one of your officials to lead him around the city. Proclaim how the King honours such men. Make him royalty for a day!'

'I like this idea.'

Haman's eyes grew wide. 'Wonderful, Your Majesty. I feel honoured that you would—'

A look of presumption shone from the Viceroy's eyes. 'Go, do it!' the King commanded.

'"Do it?" Your Majesty?'

'Do it for this man, Mordecai. Do you know him? He's a royal official here in the citadel. I would hope that Persia's Viceroy knows all his administrators.'

And at this point, a wave of confusion swept over Haman. Two separate worlds seemed to collide in his mind, and he was unsure whether they were speaking about Mordecai's execution or his honour. 'Excuse me, Your Majesty. Mordecai?'

'Yes, you do know of him, don't you?'

'I'm, I'm aware, yes.'

'Then what are you waiting for? He protected me from assassination, and we never rewarded him. I'll honour him so that others might be inspired to do likewise. Be the one to guide him through the city in the manner you described. You're my top official. What greater honour could I give the man? Send for my best horse and robes. Is that all clear?'

'I...'

Xerxes perceived Haman's pride was being offended. *Haman is a good viceroy, but I need to remind him that even my highest official is still my slave.* 'Haman, are you alright? You look ill.'

Haman's mouth moved, but words failed to emerge.

'Well if it's nothing, get to it. That's an order. Hurry up. If you're too slow, you'll miss the Queen's banquet. We wouldn't want that, now would we?'

A Persian four-letter word flashed through his mind, but his mouth uttered, 'I shall perform your command at once!' Haman bowed and left the throne room to do all the King had asked of him. He did so with a terrible foreboding that he couldn't put words to. His ambitions had run into an invisible wall that he could feel but not comprehend—and the dread of it shook him.

The Girl and the Guardian

53

THE GRANDFATHER AND grandson were within a stone's throw of the cottage. The walk had invigorated Oliver, but he was now looking forward to escaping from the wind and drinking something warm.

'The Highlands!' he exclaimed, feeling a sense of awe over his surroundings.

'What about 'em?'

'They'd be an excellent setting for my script. The hills are so simple yet dramatic.'

'I thought ye were settin' it in a war.'

'How about a war between ancient Scottish clans?'

'I prefer stories where we kill the English.'

'Cheers, grandpa.'

'Nothing personal, laddie. You're half-Scottish, we'd spare ye.'

'Glad to hear it.'

'Well, wherever ye set yer story, think about the characters first. Write a few sentences of what they'd be like and what they

The Oliver Anderson Trilogy

might represent for you—think about how they might change throughout yer story.'

'Speaking of characters, I find this Haman fella compelling.'

'How so?'

'Well, on the one hand, he seems ethical. He cares about justice—or at least his understanding of what justice might be. In some ways, I'd say he's more moral than me. Yet, he's evil.'

'Aye. It's men and women who care deeply about ethics that have committed many of this world's atrocities. Some have a strong moral compass—it's merely pointed the wrong way.'

'I'm used to thinking of wicked people as being unprincipled.'

William nodded. 'Many a wicked man or woman has offered up human lives on the altar of cherished principles.'

They arrived back, took off their wet and grassy wellies, and entered the warmth of the cottage. 'Another coffee?' William asked.

'Of course,' Oliver said as he sat down on the sofa. He looked over at his laptop and wondered what sentences he might start typing if he were to pick it up now. He was glad to be out of London. Spending time with his grandfather was helping him to think outside of boxes he didn't even know he had. *Now if I could only get a plot, some characters, and an appropriate setting together, I might accomplish what I came all this way for.*

The Girl and the Guardian

William set the mug down on the side table as his grandson stared into the void that artists look into when they need inspiration. 'Here ye go.'

'Thanks,' Oliver said as he wrapped his cold hands around the hot cup. 'If Haman thought he was doing justice but was wrong, what else are humans capable of screwing up?'

'We're gifted at doing what's bad whilst thinking it's good.'

'Go team human!'

William chuckled at his grandson. 'Exactly!'

'In college, I took a philosophy class. Sometimes the subject of Christianity came up.'

William tightened his lips. 'Hmm, I'm sure it did, though I imagine not always in the best of ways.'

'Perhaps, but some of the questions were good.'

'Such as?'

'Well, for example, what we're talking about now: justice. We were talking about Jesus' crucifixion—the Beautiful Ugly as you call it.'

'What about it?'

'A Muslim student described why Islam rejects Jesus' death from the standpoint of justice—even many of the non-religious students agreed with the objection.'

'What did the lad say?'

'He asked, "How can the temporary sufferings of one man erase the eternal punishment of humanity's billions?" He didn't think it was fair that Jesus should be able to forgive countless multitudes of people for all eternity by suffering for a few

227

hours. He also asked why Allah, God I guess, had to let Jesus suffer. Why couldn't he forgive if he was all-powerful? It didn't seem like justice to him—it seemed more like a great injustice. Doesn't he make a good point?'

'Those are two grand objections, laddie!'

'Sorry, is it too much?'

'No, Christians should never run from difficult questions. At the very least, it should make us think harder. A friend of the truth has nothing to fear from honest questioning.'

'So how would you have responded to him?'

'Justice, rightly understood, is beautiful. When ye perceive injustice, it looks ugly. Beauty in the physical world depends upon proportions, fittingness, and symmetry. Likewise, the Tree where Jesus died is beautiful because of the fittin' work of justice done on it.'

'But how was it just? It's not clear—at least not to me.'

'The Messiah became a sin offering on a Roman execution stake. He stood as a substitute for people who had committed high-treason against Heaven. Jesus let Heaven pour out its terrible justice on himself. This justice was equal in proportion to what our treason deserved. In that sense, his sacrifice was perfectly fittin'—it was beautiful in proportion.'

'It seems uneven to me.'

'This Saviour could suffer on behalf of the many—and it still be justice—because he is of so much greater value.'

The Girl and the Guardian

Oliver's eyes widened at his grandfather's words 'Jesus is worth more than millions or billions of people?! How can you say one life is greater than another?'

'Remember, laddie, who Christians believe Jesus is. We believe he's the eternal Word of God. He's the one who created the galaxies and who holds it all together. The distance between his worth and ours is greater than the distance between our worth and an ant's.'

Oliver leaned back onto the sofa, trying to get his mind around what his grandfather had said. 'It's still hard to see how God could save so many from the sacrifice of one.'

'How many ants would you sacrifice to save a human baby?'

'What?'

'Don't act confused, laddie. If you're driving yer car and it spins out of control, and there's a human baby on the left side of the road and an anthill with a million ants on the right, which way do ye swerve?'

'I don't know.'

'Yes, you do. Only in something like a philosophy class is that even close to being a hard decision. Don't be an eejit. In real life, ye would run over a thousand anthills before you ever came near a real baby.'

'Yes. I probably would. But it's hard to explain why exactly.'

'Because, contrary to whatever philosophy your school may have fed ye, deep down you know a human is of greater worth than that of an insect—even if ye lack the reasoning to explain why. In the same way, God is of far greater value than us; like a

229

painter being of more worth than her painting. That's why the One could die for the many—it was in the value of the One.'

'Okay, I can see why that's maybe fair. But couldn't a good God forgive everyone without Jesus having to die?'

'Would a good judge at the London courthouse let all of the guilty criminals go free? Is that what a "good" judge does? Or does a good judge give people what they deserve?'

Oliver opened his mouth, but no response came to mind. 'Give me a minute grandpa. I need the caffeine to kick-in.'

'Take all the time ye need, laddie. I'll take us back to Haman.'

54

HAMAN SKITTERED LIKE a cockroach through the city and into his mansion. 'Darling! Where are you? Our evening plans have changed!' Escorting Mordecai through the city on the royal horse had left the Viceroy shaken with shame but not stirred to repentance. His ego, like his voice, was hurt from repeatedly shouting out that Mordecai was the one the King honoured—hurt, but not broken.

His day, thus far, had been a long week.

'I'm right here,' Zeresh said, descending the stairs. 'My goodness! What happened to you? You're all sweaty, and your shoes are covered in dirt!'

'I'll explain later. Listen, we need to change our plans for this evening. There'll be no execution—not tonight at least.'

'Why? Is Mordecai being taken care of by other means?'

'Depends what you mean by "taken care of". Mordecai's being taken care of by Xerxes who's taken a liking to the man and has showered him with honour of the most extreme type!'

'No! How strange.'

231

'Yes! Right before I requested to have him executed, Xerxes asked me to be the instrument of having him honoured. He made me lead Mordecai around on a royal horse!' Haman said as his wife began to help him remove his dirtied robes.

'Why would he give that job to you?'

'I don't know! His tone seemed cool towards me—so different from the warmth I felt at the banquet yesterday.'

'This is bizarre! I suppose we can't execute Mordecai now—or even have him fired.'

'Exactly! We should take that stake down lest anyone ask why we've built it. If word ever got out that we were going to kill a man that the King had honoured, it could mean the end of my career as Viceroy—at the least.'

'Of course, darling. I'll have the servants take it down first thing tomorrow.' With the outer layer of Haman's robes off, Zeresh fell back on the bed and let out a giant exhale. 'We won't let this bother us. The man's not worth the wood it takes to impale him anyway.'

Haman began to put on his dinner clothes. 'That's a nice way to think of it, but Mordecai's sudden exaltation by Xerxes unnerves me.'

'How did that bug ever gain royal favour?'

'Apparently, he was involved in uncovering an assassination attempt.'

'Which one?'

'I didn't ask—there have been quite a few over the years,' Haman said, looking into a reflective glass. 'The King didn't

The Girl and the Guardian

reward him at the time, and so today—of all days!—he decides to have me shout the praises of this dirty Jew.'

'He's Jewish?'

'Mordecai?'

'Yes, Mordecai. Is he Jewish?'

'Of course. I thought you knew that.' Haman lied. He knew Zeresh, as a Persian, had little patience for his ancient family feud.

'You said he refused to bow and give you appropriate honour.'

'And that's true. That's what happened.'

'And so this had nothing to do with his ethnicity?'

Haman looked straight into his wife's eyes and lied again. 'No. Not at all.'

'I'd assumed the man was Persian. He doesn't have a Jewish name.'

'Not all Jews do—but what does it matter?'

'Are you sure this isn't about your old rivalry?'

Haman's frustrations from the day exploded onto his wife. 'You aren't an Amalekite! You won't understand it. The Jews are the reason we're no longer a great nation. They're the reason I'm a Viceroy instead of an Agag—a king in my own right! They killed my people, and they deserve all I'm preparing for them!'

'Calm down, dear! I'm not the enemy. I'm worried about you. There are stories of great reversals in Israel's history. It looks like they're about to be wiped out and then, without anyone expecting it, a great rescue comes their way.'

The Oliver Anderson Trilogy

'The Jews are far from Israel now. This isn't the land of their god.'

'The stories exist even here. You should know them. As Viceroy, you stand in the position Daniel the Jew once stood.'

'I don't need this right now!'

'Don't get angry at me. I'm trying to help. It is a bad omen to make yourself an enemy of the Jews.'

Haman realised that he was losing his self-control—a character flaw he hated. 'Look, darling, I apologise. I shouldn't be angry with you. But please know that my plans are bigger than Mordecai. Our family will finish what my ancestors started. Our sons and I will exterminate these Jews by the year's end—and then you'll never have to listen to me go on about them again.'

Zeresh sat up on the bed and stared at her husband. 'Exterminate? What are you talking about?'

'Most of the city found out four days ago when I released an official proclamation.'

'Is that how I'm supposed to learn about my husband's activities? By keeping up with all the news reports messengers bring from the palace?'

Haman ignored her objection and continued. 'We'll use the mechanisms of the Persian government and the people of this Empire to ensure that the Jews will no longer stain this earth with their existence.'

'Haman, dear, what if this backfires on us? Please rethink—'

'No! No more thinking! It's a time for action.'

The Girl and the Guardian

'Be careful. Xerxes honouring Mordecai—it's a bad sign.'

Haman looked with confidence at his anxious wife. 'I've thought through every conceivable detail and analyzed every possible obstacle to my plan. I've prepared for every contingency. No one can rescue the Jews from my hands.'

A voice boomed from the front of the house. 'The royal eunuchs have arrived to escort the Viceroy to the palace!'

'I must go now, or I'll be late.'

'I trust you. But at least think about my concerns.'

Haman leaned over and kissed his wife on the cheek. 'We can talk more if you'd like. If our sons and I succeed, we will accomplish what the Agags of our people set out to do, but were unable. I must go now. I can't keep royalty waiting.'

'Good-bye. I love you.'

'See you this evening.'

55

HAMAN BOWED TO as he turned the corner to the Queen's quarters and found the King waiting there. 'Your Majesty.'

'Haman.' Xerxes had half hoped his Viceroy would be late due to the humbling job he had assigned him. He still felt inexplicably annoyed with him even as he looked forward to the banquet he was about to enjoy with the Queen.

A eunuch raised his voice. 'His Imperial Highness and his chief servant, Haman, have arrived to dine with Her Imperial Highness, Queen Esther!' Female servants swung the door open and led them through an ornate hall to the room where they were to dine.

The maidservants lead them to the wine room—a room where the Queen entertained female guests with some of Persia's finest vintage. Items from all over the Empire graced the walls. Two large windows and an archway gave a beautiful view to one of the palace's many gardens—complete with fragrant herbs, fruit trees, and bushes all trimmed as carefully as a poodle dog. No lamps were needed as the room had more than

The Girl and the Guardian

ample sunlight. Two musicians played in the far corner: one on a stringed instrument, one on a simple drum.

Esther reclined on a couch of pillows above a slightly elevated table. She wore a simple blue robe that wrapped around her neck, revealing her brown, nubile arms, decorated with golden bracelets. Her hair was piled upon her head and held aloft by the imperial crown—save for a few ringlets framing her face. To see her lying there in her simple beauty took their breath away.

The table before her was magnificent. It exceeded even the magnificence of the day before. Sweet grape jelly, candied turnips, radishes prepared with salt, capers, herbs and dates baked on flatbread, cheeses, fruits both fresh and dried, and a variety of meats all in the finest gold and silver bowls imaginable.

The Queen smiled. 'Welcome, Haman. Welcome, Your Majesty.' She rose from her pillow and bowed before both her guests—an act that simultaneously pleased Haman and renewed the unease stirring within the King. She returned to her sofa and both men also reclined, each on a purple couch of their own.

They dined, conversed, and laughed. Freshly bathed, cinnamon skinned servants—beautiful girls and eunuch boys—walked gracefully about the room in white tunics. They carried new wines to complement the luxurious meal set before them. Xerxes released his unease, and let the wines, the food, and the Queen's graciousness sweep him away.

Haman, beginning to forget about his horrid morning, relished this second day of dining with the royal couple and began to wonder if this was going to become a regular occurrence. As the day before, Haman delighted in the Queen's attention.

Midway through the meal, and after not a few glasses of wine, Xerxes smiled and began his anticipated speech. 'Esther, my dove, you have wooed me both with your banquets and your company these last two days. Something is on your mind. Please, tell me what it is, and I will do it for you.'

Esther rose from her couch and bowed humbly once again. 'My generous Lord and King, if it makes you happy to grant any request of mine, and only if you are pleased to do so, then I ask that you would spare both my life and the life of my people from utter destruction.'

The musicians faltered. The King paused with a puzzled look—wondering if his bride was making a joke. Haman looked back and forth between the two, thinking that he had misheard.

The King, this time without a smile, spoke again. 'My dear, I'm not sure I've understood you. What do you mean by sparing your life? Do you think you're in some sort of danger?'

'I know that I am, Your Majesty.'

Her words annoyed the King. 'Do you doubt my ability to protect my own? Even now the palace is surrounded by 1,000 Immortals. You're safe,' he said, hoping that would reassure her.

But Esther continued. She had rehearsed every word and was not going to slow down or stop. 'If it were only something as

The Girl and the Guardian

small as someone selling my people and me into slavery, then I wouldn't come to you—for that would be too small a concern to trouble your mind. I assure you that I'm not joking or mistaken. I can show you proof. It's solid. Someone wants to kill me, my family, and my people.'

The moment she said this, two things happened simultaneously. The first was that an idea flashed through the deep mazes of Haman's meticulous mind. In all his dark conniving and ambitious strategizing, one possibility had never occurred to him. He had never considered that he might be outfoxed—not by a young queen.

Wait. No. It can't be.

The other thing was that Xerxes, in good Xerxes fashion, exploded in rage. He jumped to his feet. Food, wine, and a large hookah pipe flew in all directions. His face reddened. 'Who'd dare?!' he roared. 'If this is true, I'll kill the man responsible!'

His rage shook even Esther. She'd anticipated an outburst, but not of this intensity. She trembled, bowed, and then rose to point at her adversary. 'If my kind lord does wish to rescue me from my attacker, then know that the one who wants me dead is this evil Haman!'

Haman jumped to his feet. His lips danced about on his terrified face, but no words managed to escape. Bodyguards that stood in the room's dark corners grasped the handles of their swords and exchanged glances. They were conscious that a threatening situation was emerging, but were unsure where it was going. Xerxes' mind raced in uncertainty, recalling back to

The Oliver Anderson Trilogy

when Haman spoke something to him about a rebellious people, Jews, and a massive influx into the treasury. Food, wine, and naked harem girls had preoccupied his mind, and he hadn't looked closely at the details. The confusion was too much. He needed to think clearly. He stormed out a side door, and into the Queen's private garden.

Stupefied, Haman gazed at the Queen, who now sat on her couch, awful in her majesty. Her eyes locked onto his, but they were no longer warm, flirtatious, or inviting—instead, they daggered into his soul. He had lowered his guard for a young girl's pretty smile and dark eyelashes. The best-manicured hands in the Empire now held his fate—and they were the hands of a Jewess.

Haman threw himself on her couch. 'Your Majesty, I didn't know.'

Esther said nothing. Her stare bound his eyes to hers and forbade him to turn away.

'Please spare my life!'

Esther never responded. She didn't have to. At that moment, the King of kings re-entered the room just as Haman was extending his hand to the Queen's feet. The jealous seed Esther had planted deep in his mind the day before now erupted into its intended volcanic action.

'You'd make a cuckold out of me?!' The King roared. The bodyguards understood enough. They tackled, bound, and covered Haman's head with a hood. As if proof of hell and divine judgment, the last thing Haman ever saw, as he turned

240

his gaze from the King, was a Jewish girl blowing him a kiss good-bye.

Xerxes put his foot on the neck of Haman's hooded and bound body. 'Any man who touches the Queen must die!'

Hathach, who was standing in attendance to the King, bowed. 'Your Majesty, Haman built a seventy-five-foot pole on which to impale Mordecai, the man who helped save you from assassins. It is at his house.'

'What?! Well, throw him on it then!' The King pronounced. And off they took Haman to the worst of all deaths: the death a man creates for himself.

"Who is he, and where is he, who has dared to do this?"
And Esther said, "A foe and enemy! This wicked Haman!"
Then Haman was terrified before the king and the queen.

-Esther 7

The Girl and the Guardian

56

THE IMMORTALS IMPALED Haman's bound body on the high spike he had crafted the night before. The realization of his impending death caught him unprepared. He had plans. His life had been going somewhere important—or so he had thought. He realized that his soul was about to be dispatched into the mystery. Questions bounced hysterically off the walls of his mind: Will I face oblivion or eternity? Will I meet anyone there? Pure terror, 200 proof, was injected right into his soul as he began, even now, to feel the flames of what awaited him on the other side of life's curtain.

The elite warriors watched as this damned Agag thrashed in a shower of his own blood. Gore ran down the spike and puddled at their feet while Haman's wife and sons watched in horror from the house. Once all life had departed from his kebabbed corpse, they reported back to the King and Queen who were still in the Queen's reception room. Upon hearing the news, Esther's heart shifted gears. Like a mama tiger calming herself when a predator is removed from her offspring, so her rage against Israel's adversary subsided. Esther fell and began to wet Xerxes' feet with her tears.

'My King. Please. A word from you and my people will be safe.'

Xerxes was slow to speak as his mind processed all that was happening. He guessed that this whole situation had been made possible because of his negligence. He put a hand on her shoulder. 'It's not that simple. One cannot revoke a law given by the King—not even the King himself can do that. But, still, we may be able to do something.'

Xerxes took Esther's hand and lifted her. They sat on one of the sofas and began to talk—a phenomenon that was not a regular occurrence in their marriage. Esther began to open up and share her background with her husband for the first time. He stared at her with genuine care—something he had not done since they were first married. He bathed her in his attention, and it thrilled her.

When she told him about Mordecai, Xerxes was surprised. 'The man who saved me? Your informant? That's your father?'

'My adopted father, Your Majesty.'

'I now understand why he brought the information to you— and why you would trust him.' Xerxes turned to Hathach. 'Bring him here at once. I may have a promotion for him.'

Hathach bowed. 'Yes, Your Majesty.'

Turning back to Esther, he asked, 'Has it been long since you've seen him?'

'Almost five years, my lord.'

And so, Xerxes brought his servant before him, and Esther was reunited with Mordecai. As her adopted father, Mordecai was permitted to touch the Queen. They didn't so much embrace as clench each other.

Under other circumstances, such a reunion might have led to a celebration. But these were not normal circumstances. Xerxes promoted Mordecai, right there and then, to the now-vacant position of Viceroy. It was a snap decision that sent shockwaves through political chatter of the citadel and came as no small surprise to the two cousins. It was in his newly appointed position as Viceroy that the King took counsel with Mordecai, and discussed how to rescue the Jews.

'I think you understand, my young Viceroy. Haman's edict cannot be revoked—lest the entire Persian legal system collapse. Your people must face genocide. But that doesn't mean you're helpless.'

'The Jews have never been helpless, Your Majesty. We've always had a Rescuer. In any case, I have a plan.'

The Queen sat on her couch, listening, in near disbelief. She watched Xerxes and Mordecai strategised together. It was surreal—as if her past life as a Jewish commoner and her new life as the Persian Queen had merged. But, if she thought that catch-ups and leisurely walks in the garden with these two men on either side of her would be what filled up her next few weeks, she was mistaken. There was work to be done.

245

57

THE QUEEN LOOKED hesitantly at her new Viceroy as they stood in one of the palace's stately rooms. Several scrolls were by his side, and he held tight to his quill as if it were a sword. 'There isn't enough perfume in all of Persia to erase the stench of Haman's lust for glory. Are you sure you're willing to accept the responsibility for his filthy estate?'

'Only if you're asking.'

'I am—but only if you're sure it's not too much. With Haman and his sons being as dead as a doorknob, someone has to do it. Xerxes gave it to me, but I don't know where to begin managing all that land and wealth.'

Mordecai bowed towards his cousin with a smile. 'Let me take it from you, Your Majesty.'

'Why do they call it that anyway?'

'What?'

'"Dead as a doorknob". Why is a doorknob thought to be especially dead?'

'Have you ever seen a living doorknob?'

The Girl and the Guardian

'Funny. Don't you have an Empire or something to run Mr.Viceroy?'

'That and an estate my cousin just dumped on me.'

'Morty! If you don't want it, say so!'

Mordecai grinned. 'Calm down. I'll take it.' He had missed these conversations. 'In any case, it'll be a reminder to me of where ambition can lead a man. I'm a son of Adam like him and could get consumed with the same drive for gold, glory, and revenge. May Heaven keep me from using this new position to serve myself!'

Esther smiled at her old mentor. 'That's a good prayer.'

'How did Daniel, Abednego, and the others keep their sanity at the heights of such power?'

'You have me. I'll give you a good kick if you get too big-headed. I'm the Queen. I can do that now, you know,' she said with a wink. 'But, seriously, you're nothing like Haman.'

'But I can become like him. A man who sets out to make his people great can soon start living to make himself great. Haman's life showed me the road to hell—may Heaven help me walk a different way.'

Esther approached her older cousin and pressed her hand against his heart. 'You were once a great guardian over me. I know you'll be a faithful guardian for our people.' With that, she stood on her toes, leaned forward, and kissed his cheek.

Mordecai nodded, smiled, and blushed just a bit beneath his beard. 'I'll try, Your Majesty.'

'How's our mission coming along?' Esther said, shifting the conversation back to business.

'As you see, we are writing letters on both tablets and scrolls in the King's name. These letters grant full permission for our people to make, buy, and stockpile as many weapons as they can—to defend themselves on the thirteenth day of Adar.'

'We might be the only two Jews who don't need a sword.'

'Yes—not all Jews have a thousand Immortal bodyguards protecting them. Still, it might not hurt if even we have one by our side on the day. As you know, not even this palace is safe from treason. It won't be illegal for anyone, even a bodyguard, to kill any Jew, including us on that day.'

Esther's face turned pale, and her breath faltered. 'Even us?'

'Even for us. Here, I brought you something,' Mordecai said, handing Esther an item enveloped in cloth.

She unwrapped it. 'My old dagger!'

'I doubted, as Queen, that you would ever need this again. But it'll be worth wearing on the day. Do you remember how to wield it?'

'Thank you! Yes, I think I do!' she said with a grin. She held the handle tightly and waved the weapon to and fro.

'You look fierce enough, Your Majesty. But I pray you won't ever have to use it. I'll have my cutlass and personally vet the bodyguards who surround us to ensure personal loyalty.'

Esther inserted the dagger back in its sheath. 'Morty...do you think we have a chance?'

The Girl and the Guardian

'Most Jews know little about genuine battle. We have a lot of training to do in preparation. But, yes. I think we have more than a chance. We have good people helping us. I've done all I can to strike fear into the hearts of local governors so that they'll lend support. Plus, conversions are happening.'

'What?'

'Conversions. You know, people becoming Jews.'

The news surprised her. 'Why, when, how?'

'All over the Empire. People are hearing about this great reversal and believe that only Heaven could've done such a thing. It's only a trickle now. But, if we succeed on the day, it will become a flood.'

'Whole groups of people becoming Jews? I've only ever heard of individuals—or families at the most.'

'The great rescue Heaven gave us hasn't only been for the good of the Jews. Heaven cares for all nations. Remember?'

Esther smiled. 'You may have mentioned something like that to me when I was younger.'

Just then, Hathach walked into the room. 'Your Majesty, Your Excellency.'

Mordecai turned to him. 'Hathach, good to see you. I have several scrolls ready to go. Can you get these to the riders?'

'Of course, Your Excellency,' he said as he reached out to take five of the scrolls laying on the table.

Esther suddenly remembered something. 'Wait a minute, Hatach.'

'Yes, Your Majesty?'

'Before you go, could you tell us more about what you said to me on the day I approached the King? I told Mordecai about your encouragement, but he was as bewildered about this prophecy as I was.'

Mordecai nodded. 'Yes. With all that is going on, I had forgotten to ask. What was that about?'

'As you know, your prophet, Daniel, was once appointed by the great Babylonian King to oversee our order. He was both one of us and not one of us. After he died, we received a letter that he had written specifically for the magi. In it, he spoke of a star-child that would bring a great rescue to the nations.'

'A star-child? You mean like my name? "Esther"?'

'The prophecy spoke of a royal child who would be born under a star and who would rescue the nations from a great dragon.'

'And the Magi believe this to be the Queen?' Mordecai said with a furrowed brow.

'We do not know. Daniel's prophecies were often mysterious and sometimes had layers of meaning.'

Esther turned to Mordecai. 'Did Daniel speak of me?'

Mordecai rubbed his chin. 'I don't know. As you say Hathach, sometimes Heaven speaks in mysteries, and there can be more than one event to which a prophecy points. I am sure you were destined to play the role you have, cousin. Yet I would not want the Magi to stop contemplating what this star-child prophecy might be about. It may yet have another layer of fulfilment. This world has dragons greater than Haman.'

The Girl and the Guardian

Hathach bowed. 'It does indeed. You speak with great wisdom, Your Excellency. Shall I take the scrolls now?'

'Yes, please. We shall delay you no further.'

As Hathach turned and left, Esther looked at her cousin. 'Something to consider, huh?'

'There's much about the prophecies of Heaven that I do not understand. But I know this much: Heaven blesses us and sets us on a mission to bless others.'

Esther nodded. 'Yes, you always taught me that Israel is best when Israel lives for something other than Israel.'

'Exactly. Promised star-child or not, we must live for the glory of our God and the good of his whole world.'

'Indeed. That's something I didn't understand when I was fifteen.'

'Glad you're growing in wisdom. But before we can bless others, we must ensure they don't kill us first!'

Esther nodded her head. 'You keep writing. I'll practice with my dagger.'

The Oliver Anderson Trilogy

Then he sent the letters by mounted couriers riding on swift horses that were used in the king's service, bred from the royal stud, saying that the king allowed the Jews who were in every city to gather and defend their lives, to destroy, to kill, and to annihilate any armed force of any people or province that might attack them.

-Esther 8

The Girl and the Guardian

58

OLIVER LOOKED UP from his mug with curiosity. 'Grandpa, did that part happen? Is it in the Bible?'

'Which part are ye referring to?'

'The conversions of non-Jews.'

'Aye. It's in there. After the reversal of fortunes, there were mass conversions throughout the Persian Empire. Ye should read the real story of Esther in the Bible. It'll only take ye about half an hour.'

'I think I will—after I write my script.'

'Glad to hear.'

'What was your conversion like?'

William adjusted himself in his chair, and his eyes rolled back. 'It started with yer grandma. I didn't welcome the news of her becomin' a believer. Not only did I think that she'd hit the bottom of crazy, I thought she'd entered crazy's underground basement! She invited me to church, but I refused.'

'I guess something happened that changed your mind.'

'Well she got sweeter and kinder as a result—but it only made me angrier. I was three gallons of mean in a two-gallon

The Oliver Anderson Trilogy

bucket, and she had to clean up the mess. She did so with incredible patience. I gave up eventually—fightin' against liquid love took too much energy. I went to church with my arms crossed, but, as I was there, I listened. Finally, I knew something was missin' in my life. I was a creature that was far from his Creator, and I too bowed the knee to the Rescuer.'

'By Rescuer, you mean Jesus?'

William nodded. 'Aye, that's the One. The truer Esther.'

'What's Jesus have to do with Esther?'

'Jews and Christians both agree that the Scriptures point to the Messiah. Where we disagree is on whether Jesus, or Yeshua as they'd say in Hebrew, was the Messiah. Most Jews, religious ones anyway, are still looking for a future Messiah—though some trust in Yeshua. Christians believe he's already come.'

'How does the story of Esther point to Jesus?'

'In so many ways. Both Esther and Jesus were adopted—by Mordecai and Joseph, respectively. Esther was a child whose name meant 'star' and lived among the magi; Jesus was a child born under a star that led the Magi to him. The people around Esther were unaware of her Jewish identity; the people around Jesus were unaware of his Messianic identity. Esther humbled herself with fasting in a palace while Jesus humbled himself with fasting in a desert. Esther interceded for the Jews before the Persian King. Jesus interceded for all the nations before Heaven's King. Esther gave the Jews the feast of Purim to commemorate their redemption; Jesus gave his followers the Lord's Supper to celebrate theirs. Esther risked the wrath of an

The Girl and the Guardian

earthly king; Jesus bore the wrath of the Heavenly King. The King elevated Esther, a commoner, to a throne; God elevated Jesus, a poor wandering Rabbi, to Heaven's throne.'

'Wow, there are interesting similarities.'

'There's an important difference, ye see,' William was quick to add. 'Esther was born with external beauty that she used, but Jesus gave up his eternal beauty so that we could have true beauty before God.'

'The Beautiful Ugly?'

'Aye.'

'So Christians see Jesus as giving them victory like Mordecai and Esther did to the Jews—only a spiritual one. Is that right?'

'Aye. If it's true, this story is the greatest one ever told.'

'Grandpa, I don't know if what you believe about the Beautiful Ugly and Jesus' resurrection is true, but it *is* lovely.'

'Bach, Handel, Michaelangelo, Dostoevsky—many great artists have found their inspiration in the Bible generally and in Jesus specifically over the centuries.'

'I feel something stirring inside me for this script now, but it's not quite there yet.'

'I'll pray for you, laddie. Perhaps with a good night's sleep, you'll have greater clarity in the morning.'

'Thanks. So?'

'So?'

'Mordecai and Esther. Did they live happily ever after?'

'Ah, yes. Let's see what happens.'

59

THEY STOOD ON the Queen's palace balcony. Her hand perched on his shoulder like a bird surveying the city. The cousins admired the urban view in front of them while the morning sun shone on the city and bathed it afresh in golden warmth. The Queen took a sip of cool, fermented milk and turned towards her the Viceroy. 'Come and eat.'

They made their way to the well-laid table. Hadassah smiled. 'Our meal, like justice, has been served.'

'Justice?' Mordecai replied. 'How so?'

'How? Haman, his sons, and our enemies are defeated. Our people throughout the Empire are celebrating.'

'I see that as an act of mercy more than justice.'

'You're not suggesting it would've been just if Haman had destroyed us?'

'No, Your Majesty. All I'm saying is that justice is always a double-edged sword. The whole reason Heaven exiled us to Babylon in the first place is that we acted wickedly. Perfect justice for the world might look far uglier than what you care to imagine. Heaven save us from getting what we all deserve!'

256

'When you put it like that, yes, Heaven has been merciful to us.'

'I think it was merciful enough to offer even Haman a chance to repent. At least, that's what I felt the day he was forced to give me a horseback tour of the city. By the end, I pitied the poor creature.'

'Pity? If a son of Adam ever deserved impaling, it was Haman.'

'Perhaps. But I'd rather not sit as judge over such matters.'

'Well, whether it's justice or mercy, at least our people are safe.'

'Yes. For the time.'

'Only "for the time"?'

'There are some evils that even the grave doesn't bury. Darkness will find a home in other powerful rulers. Our people will be in dire straights and look destruction in the eyes yet again.'

'Will we never be safe?'

'We will be when the Messiah comes.'

'Will he destroy all our enemies?'

'Better. He'll destroy enmity itself.'

'How?'

'Not even the prophets know.'

'Will he have to go through the same sort of loneliness, pain, and anguish we did?'

Mordecai mused. 'Will the Messiah suffer? What a question! But I'm afraid it's one that's above this Viceroy's paygrade. As for you and me, yes, it certainly did feel like a series of unfortunate events victimised us.'

Esther smiled. 'Yes, but Heaven brought good from evil.'

'It did. The stories of Scripture are now our story—and you played a role in it.'

'As did you, dear Viceroy. Somehow we both escaped death.'

'You might be doomed to live after all.'

'Poor me!' Esther laughed as she picked up a piece of cheese with her bread and took a bite. After swallowing she took a deep breath and asked, 'What do you think my parents would've thought about all this?'

Mordecai looked across the table and saw both the regal woman and the nine-year-old orphan at once. She was elegant and fierce—yet her eyes still carried a childhood vulnerability. 'I know Uncle Abihail would've been proud of you; as am I,' he said with sincerity.

She reached over and grasped his hand. 'Thank you.'

Mordecai reciprocated the squeeze. 'Though he would've been shocked, I'm sure!'

'About which part?'

Mordecai laughed. 'Which part wouldn't he have been shocked over? Your dad dreamt of returning to Israel. To see you now as Empress over the gentiles, that would've been outside his box.'

'It was outside my box. It was outside everyone's box!'

'Having those boxes broken wasn't exactly comfortable.'

The Girl and the Guardian

'Yes,' Esther nodded, 'but now I can see how Heaven used those experiences to bring about redemption.'

'Some years ask questions. Other years answer them.'

Esther grinned. 'You know, before all this began, I was about to insist that you find a husband for me.'

'Providence has taken care of that one,' Mordecai said with a grin. 'I don't think I would've handled the interview process particularly well.'

'I'm sure you would've fumbled your way through it.'

'Thanks for the vote of confidence, Your Majesty.'

'Heaven did save you the pains of having to find me a husband, but the one he found for me, well, it certainly was an interesting choice.'

'Don't all girls dream of marrying a prince or a king? I'm sure many women would love to be you.'

'Maybe. But it looks different from the other side.'

Mordecai smiled playfully 'Would you have preferred that I married you off to Jere instead?'

Esther choked on her food. 'What? The weird one? No, thanks!'

'I'll let him know you remember him so fondly.'

'Women may envy my beauty, but sometimes it seems like a mask—for that's all this world wants to see. They may also envy my position, but they don't have husbands who spend countless days in a harem.'

259

The Oliver Anderson Trilogy

'The kings and powerful men of the earth have always found harems a beautiful place to be. Even King Solomon had a large harem.'

'The bottom of the sea may be a beautiful place, but if a man stays there too long, he drowns. Beauty can bless, but it also deceives. Plus, at this rate, I don't know if I'll ever be pregnant.' Hadassah paused. She knew that sharing one's grief over a problematic marriage isn't easy when one's spouse is an Emperor.

'Some things are best left unsaid, Your Majesty. Especially given your circumstances. Just know that your feelings aren't a closed book to me.'

'I do,' she said with grateful eyes and turned to look towards the Jewish quarter. 'Sometimes I wish we could live in our old neighbourhood.'

'A clever girl once told me that home isn't where you're born—it's where you belong.'

'She sounds like a genius.'

Mordecai shifted his weight as he gathered his next words. 'There's another matter.'

'What's that?'

'Perhaps we could talk about my wife.'

Esther nearly dropped her cup. 'What?!' She hadn't given much thought to Mordecai's romantic life in years. 'You're married?'

'No! Or, at least, not yet. Sorry—should we talk about this another time?'

The Girl and the Guardian

'No. I mean, yes! I mean … we can talk about it now. I'm married. Why not you? It shouldn't be hard to get you hitched. You're the new Viceroy, you're single, and you don't scrub up too badly. The birds are yours for the catching, Morty! Shall we make a list of potential prospects?'

'No need. I've already found one. I've gotten engaged.'

'Shut up! You've done what? Engaged?! You got engaged without me knowing?'

'Calm down.'

'Calm down?! My best friend is engaged, and I didn't even know you were seeing anyone? I was supposed to coach you through all this and give you my wonderful advice! After all, what do you know about women?'

'I know you were hoping I'd have an awkward dating phase you could comment on. Sorry. But this courtship's been speedy—just over the last few weeks.'

'Haven't you been overseeing battles and the near genocide of our people over the last few weeks? How did you have time.'

'I never had time. That was always my problem. A few weeks ago, a prospect arose, amidst all the craziness, and I took it.'

His word's failed to placate the Queen. 'A few weeks, huh? Well, tell me then. Who is she? Anyone I know from synagogue?'

'No. She wasn't at synagogue when you were there. But it is someone you've met.'

'Well, who?'

'Sabina.'

'Sabina who?'

'Sabina, Sabina.'

'Wait... as in, Sabina?!'

He grinned. 'Yes, that Sabina.'

'I didn't realise you knew her. I thought she was engaged to—'

'One of Haman's sons? Aridai?'

'Yes.'

'Her father called it off after Haman was disgraced.'

'That makes sense.'

'There's also the matter of Aridai, like the rest of Haman's sons, being killed in the battle. But that was after the engagement was called off.'

Esther took a deep breath as compassion for her old friend emerged. 'I failed to connect the dots. Yes, her fiancé would be dead now. I hope she's okay.'

'Well, I'm hoping she's happy with her new fiancé!'

'Yes, Morty, of course. I didn't mean—'

'I know,' Mordecai interrupted. 'It's been a crazy time for her. Hopefully, she'll find the days ahead an improvement.'

'I'm sure she will, Morty. You're a great catch.'

'She tells me that you two have spent time together.'

Hadassah swallowed. 'Oh? Did she? Well, yes, we met up a few times after they made me Queen. But it's been a while.' She spoke calmly but knew that her face was turning red as the memory of their last encounter in the hammam flashed before her.

262

'Shall I assume I have your approval?'

'My approval? You don't need my approval Morty.'

'You're the Queen, and I'm Persia's Viceroy—a formal approval is expected. But, as your friend, I'd like your approval even without the formalities. How do you feel about my choice?'

'You really want my thoughts?'

'Of course.'

'Okay.' Esther straightened up, wanting to take her friendship duty seriously. 'Why aren't you marrying a Jewish girl then? Jews should marry Jews.'

Mordecai laughed. 'You're one to talk.'

'Really? You're going there, huh? That was under totally—'

'—different circumstances. I know.' He grinned. 'To address your pointed and thoughtful question, don't worry. She's converted.'

'Converted?'

'Yes, she joined some of the other gentiles yesterday in a ceremony. I witnessed her baptism. It was only then that our engagement became formal.'

'Sabina…converted?'

'You're shocked that the same Heaven who rescued our people from Egypt and Haman can also rescue a girl from sin?'

'So, she knows what she's doing? I mean, she knows the law of Moses?'

'In preparation for her baptism, she had the Torah read to her. A Persian translation, of course.'

The Oliver Anderson Trilogy

'Why pick her?'

'Why do I want to marry her?'

'Yeah. Why?' Esther pressed the question.

'Well, um…have you seen her?'

'More than you know,' she said with a mischievous grin.

Mordecai looked a bit confused. 'Is that a "yes"?'

'Yes, I've seen her.'

Mordecai flashed a laddish grin. 'Well, she's hot.'

'Men!' Esther exclaimed, rolling her eyes.

'Guilty as charged.'

'Okay, perhaps she is hot,' Esther confessed. 'You're in for a treat on your wedding night, Morty! No!—don't ask what I mean by that. But, and here's my point, there's got to be more than looks. Just because a girl is a fun weekend binge, it hardly means that she'll be any good as a steady diet.'

'Wise words. And, yes, there's more. Part of it is admittedly political—her parents are aristocrats. On a personal note, I'm moved by her conversion. Her parents allowed it, but they didn't join her in this. She embraced our faith alone.'

Esther raised her eyebrows. 'So, she's serious then?'

'Yes, I'm sure of it. Are you okay? You seem more shaken by my news than I anticipated.'

'It's all so much…I don't know—'

'Change?'

'Yes. Change,' Esther reached over and placed her hand on his again. 'It's good to have you back. Every Queen needs a constant; someone who can finish her sentences and tell her

The Girl and the Guardian

things about herself that even she doesn't know. She needs someone who knows her inside and out and still loves her. You do a great job of being that person.'

'One tries one's best,' he said, gratefully. 'Change is part of growing up. I'm no longer your guardian—not officially. You're an adult. You have a husband. You're the Queen! I love you Hadassah, and will always be here for you. My upcoming marriage won't change that. After all, you and I have work to do together. Persia needs reform and Israel needs protection.'

Esther hesitated. 'The last time a big change came into my life, it was in the form of a kidnapping. I know Heaven can bring good out of the bad, but I'd like just a bit of stability.'

Mordecai looked at her with his kind eyes.

She couldn't refuse him. 'Fine! You have my approval. I give you my blessing as your Queen and as your friend. Marry the girl. Make sure you have a hammam in your house.'

Mordecai gave a small bow, knowing those words had cost her something. 'Thank you. I'm glad to hear it.'

'Change… here we come! Tell Sabina to give me time. It'll be strange to have her as part of our family.'

'As you wish, Your Majesty.'

'That's getting old. When it's just the two of us, you can call me Hadassah.'

'I'll make a note of it, Your Majesty.'

She grabbed a fig from the table and threw it at him. 'Obnoxious man!'

The Oliver Anderson Trilogy

EPILOGUE

ON THE SECOND night with his grandfather, Oliver tossed and turned in the grip of a vivid dream. In it, a small, outdoor fountain was sprouting water. As he watched, the fountain overflowed into a stream, and then into a mighty river. On both sides of the river, there grew trees that healed anyone who ate their fruit.

Then, two dragons appeared. The larger dragon tried to devour the river whilst the smaller dragon, fought to protect it. The whole world gathered to watch the fight.

At first, the bigger dragon seemed likely to win. It injured the smaller dragon, causing it to bleed into the river. But the smaller one ate of the fruit of the river's trees and was raised back up again. He continued to fight the big one with greater strength than before. Finally, the smaller dragon tore the wings off the larger one and forced it to the ground where it crushed the head of its adversary. When it won, many of those who had watched rushed to the smaller dragon and shouted its victory.

Oliver awoke with sweat on his back. 'Whoa!' he muttered. *Did I drink too much from grandpa's cask last night?* He sat in his

The Girl and the Guardian

bed and thought for some time. He wasn't used to dreams that vivid or detailed. He wondered what to do with it.

A thought came. *Pray about it.* At first, he dismissed the idea. It had been a long time since he last prayed. If he were to ever start again, he didn't want to do so over something as silly as a dream. But the dream had confused him, and the thought returned. *Pray about it.* Again, he refused.

He lay back down to sleep, but all he could think about were the dragons, the trees, and the water. He grappled over what it might mean—or if it meant anything.

Finally, as sleep continued to elude him, he sat up again. He opened his mouth and offered up a quiet prayer into the spiritual void—unsure if there was a Heaven on the receiving end or not. When he was done, he lay back down and fell into a deep sleep.

Oliver awoke again before dawn. His grandfather was still asleep. He made some black coffee and set it on the old wooden table where he sat down, opened his laptop, and typed 'The Fountain and the Dragon, by Oliver Anderson'.

Oliver wrote for three hours straight before stopping to join his grandfather for breakfast and then went back to writing. He took a brief walk with him in the afternoon, but, otherwise, Oliver was glued to the kitchen table for the whole day—with his grandfather only occasionally interrupting him to give him more food or coffee.

By evening, he had finished his script.

The next morning, William drove his grandson to the train station, where he boarded the train back to London. Oliver stepped onto the train with a firmer stride than he had when he stepped off it just three days earlier. He had received a vision and written it down with a determination to beautify the ugly.

The brakes released, and the train began towards the city.

Thank you for reading. Now what?

Indie-Authors like me depend on you. If you've enjoyed this book, please leave a review on Amazon and share it on social media with #GirlAndGuardian. Happy to hear from you at Read@JoshuaDJones.com.

The Oliver Anderson trilogy continues in...

The Genesis Ghosts

(a preview)

WE WAITED IN silence as twilight settled on our village. Sitting in my chair, I forced my lungs to breathe slowly. *Should I make a run for it?* I mused. If I ran, I'd be safe. But then I'd be a nobody. If I risked it all, I would have more honour and wealth than anyone in my family. That, or I'd be dead.

My hands trembled. The men were on their way. The identification, laid on the table in front of me, was my only hope of winning. That was my only chance of salvation and significance. For six months, I hadn't allowed those items out of my sight. They alone could restore me to riches.

'Don't be afraid,' I reassured the girl sitting across from me. 'They're not coming for you; just me.' That wasn't entirely true. It wasn't 'just' me. I placed my hand on my large bulge of a belly. *They're coming for you too.* I looked back up to the girl. 'When they arrive, just take these items to the man in charge along with the message I gave you. Can you do that?'

She thought for a moment and nodded, 'Yes.' The girl knew enough to be nervous and still chose bravery. Knowing all the

270

facts would have terrified her—as it did me. If this all went wrong, they'd most likely let her go. It's me he wanted.

It was then that the sound of angry voices floated in on the wind. The baby's father was almost here—along with the men he had gathered to murder me. *Do I stay or run?* I breathed deeply and recommitted myself to the plan. I would see this through. The time to find out if this strategy worked had arrived. The next fifteen minutes would determine whether glory or death would be mine.

The voices soon became distinguishable. It was the loud way men speak when drunk. *So, he's gathered a mob the easy way. Is my death only worth a barrel of beer to him?* I asked myself. But I knew the answer. *No, it's worth far more than that.* If my plan didn't work, then my father-in-law, the father of this baby, would spare no expense to kill me. He feared me. He believed I was channelling his brother's ghost—the brother he'd killed.

'Open up!' a voice yelled. 'Come and face the fire!'

Oliver's looked across the table with eyes the size of apples. 'What happened then?!'

'Just a mo. Ya have a light?' Tamar asked, fiddling with her plastic lighter. 'Mine's outta fluid, and I need another smoke.'

271

Other books by this author

Elijah Men Eat Meat (non-fiction) a book of short, punchy readings, following the life of Elijah, Jezebel, and Ahab. Great as a devotional.

Forbidden Friendships (non-fiction) a pastoral discussion on the subject of platonic friendships between men and women in the church.

The Cross and The Cannibal (non-fiction) a short e-book on cannibalism, the Hannibal series, and Christian orthodoxy

and…

And soon to arrive, *The Genesis Ghosts*, the second novel in **The Oliver Anderson Trilogy**—a dark fantasy is built around the Biblical epic of Judah, Tamar, and Joseph.

Printed in Great Britain
by Amazon